Moonshell

*Also by Bea Carlton
in Large Print:*

In the House of the Enemy

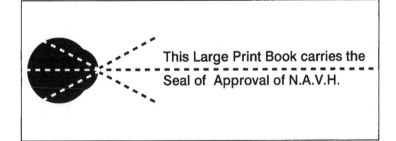

Moonshell

Bea Carlton

Thorndike Press • Waterville, Maine

Published in 2002 by arrangement with Bea Carlton.

Thorndike Press Large Print Christian Mystery Series.

The tree indicium is a trademark of Thorndike Press.

The text of this Large Print edition is unabridged.
Other aspects of the book may vary from the original edition.

Set in 16 pt. Plantin by Elena Picard.

Printed in the United States on permanent paper.

Library of Congress Cataloging-in-Publication Data

Carlton, Bea.
    Moonshell / Bea Carlton.
      p. cm.
    ISBN 0-7862-4540-9 (lg. print : hc : alk. paper)
    1. Antiquities — Collection and preservation — Fiction.
2. Mayas — Antiquities — Fiction. 3. Texas — Fiction.
4. Large type books. I. Title.
PS3553.A736 M6 2002
813′.54—dc21   2002028620

*Lovingly dedicated to my mother,
Linnie Eunice Harris,
the first Linn in my life.*

1

Weeks later Linn Randolph would look back and remember the day the strange and terrifying happenings first stalked the corridors of Moonshell. It started off just like any ordinary day.

Linn and her thirteen-year-old sister, Penny Marshall, had been far down the beach that morning, searching for new specimens to add to their rapidly growing shell collection. The sun was nearly overhead as they returned home, exultant over their newfound treasures but weary and hungry.

Linn could not remember a time in her life when she had felt more carefree and happy than in the two weeks they had been at Moonshell. The sun, the surging surf, the fishing, boating and sightseeing were all they could want.

As they began the gentle ascent toward Moonshell, Penny darted on ahead, carrying her plastic pail of newly acquired shells. Almost as if he had been watching for her, Alfred Benholt, the housekeeper's thin, fifteen-year-old son, moved out of the path near the south side of the house and joined her.

Linn stopped and watched them, an odd feeling of unease touching her. She should be pleased, she supposed, that there was someone here who was near Penny's age. But there was something about the intense, dark-headed Benholt boy that Linn distrusted. The intelligent brown eyes, framed in horn-rimmed glasses, had a look of seriousness and maturity that didn't seem to fit his lean, long, somewhat awkward body. And he had seemed completely enthralled with Penny from the moment he had laid eyes on her.

Linn grimaced. Could her distrust be only over-protectiveness? She considered the possibility and the reasons. Perhaps. Penny was Linn's only sister and growing up fast.

Penny had been a skinny kid, all legs like a young colt, when she and Aunt Kate had come to live with Linn and her husband, Clay, two years before. Now Penny had a slim, trim figure softly rounding into young womanhood. Linn had observed that although not beautiful, her appealing, pointed face so like Linn's, dancing green eyes and shining, pale blond hair were already causing young male heads to turn for a second look.

Linn, who had been placed in an orphanage when her mother died in a tuberculosis sanitarium, had not even known she had a sister until two years ago when her Aunt Kate had confessed to taking her sister's newborn baby to raise as her own when it was left an orphan. It had been a great joy to both Linn and Penny to discover they were not only cousins but also sisters.

Penny and Alfred had now disappeared down the path and were hidden from Linn's view. She moved quickly up the slope until she could see down the path to her left. Penny and Alfred were sitting together at a small, white lawn table, the blond and dark heads almost touching as they examined the shells Penny had collected, and which Linn could see were now spread out over the table.

Linn silently scolded herself. Alfred seemed a nice boy and he was just two years older than Penny. And Penny liked him. *I'll have to watch myself,* Linn thought ruefully, *or I'll be trying to run Penny's life.*

She turned away and proceeded toward the house, stopping after a few steps to survey Moonshell in the bright morning sunlight. Delight registered in her expressive, pointed face and startlingly green, gold-flecked eyes.

Clay had not exaggerated Moonshell's beauty, she thought. The mansion was round like a huge globe, with a porch running completely around the ground floor, supported by gracefully carved pillars. A balustraded balcony, boasting the same ornate columns, encircled the second story. A circular tower with a parapeted widow's walk crowned the top of the roof. The glistening white building looked for all the world like a mammoth, glossy white milky moon shell.

"Beautiful," Linn breathed, almost in awe.

Linn stepped onto a sidewalk, bordered on each side with well-tended flower beds, and started toward the front door. She suddenly came upon Joe Benholt, Alfred's older brother, working on his knees in a flower bed next to the house. Joe greeted her in a friendly manner and went on with his work. Linn walked on, remembering how she and Clay had first met the twenty-three-year-old Benholt twins in Idaho a few months before when they were in their fourth year of medical school.

Although twins, Joe and Josie looked nothing alike. Joe was about five foot ten and had curly dark brown hair. Josie was a petite five foot, with a dark complexion and black hair as straight as Joe's was curly. Her dark brown eyes were shy — in fact, she reminded Linn of a gentle-eyed doe, uneasy and poised for flight — while her brother's hazel eyes were direct, almost challenging, at times.

As Linn mounted the steps, she recalled how Joe had told Clay that the Moonshell owner, Clyde Cameron, was selling his partly finished shopping center near the Gulf of Mexico, in Corpus Christi, Texas, for a very good price. As the owner and operator of the Randolph Realty and Development Company, Clay had begun negotiations with Clyde Cameron right away.

But soon Clay had confided to Linn that he and Clyde couldn't seem to agree on anything. Every tiny word and clause of the contract seemed to require days, even weeks, to resolve. Finally Clay had wearily and regretfully told Linn that it looked like a real vacation was out of the question for the Randolphs this summer. It appeared that negotiations were going to drag on interminably.

So it still seemed like a delightful dream that they were here in Texas, at this elegantly beautiful, luxuriously furnished mansion on Aransas Bay. Linn moved on into the house, still musing at how this glorious, full summer vacation had materialized so suddenly.

Clyde Cameron had abruptly decided to spend the summer in Ireland. Needing finances quickly, he had suddenly turned amicable. He had agreed to Clay's terms, throwing in the rent-free use of his lovely coastal home, Moonshell, for the whole summer as an added inducement if the deal could be consummated quickly.

Clay had snapped up the offer.

So Clay had moved his family here for the summer. Eric Ford, Clay's top assistant in the business as well as his closest friend, had come along to help in the new enterprise. Aunt Kate and Penny had, of course, been included in the summer plans.

As Linn climbed the gracefully curving front stairs to the second floor, her mind recalled vividly how sick and emaciated Aunt Kate had been two years ago when Clay and Linn prevailed upon her to come to live with them at Grey Oaks, the huge

Randolph home in Idaho. Eleven-year-old Penny had been almost as thin.

Linn's throat constricted painfully. If only she had known their plight earlier! But it was doubtful, she knew, that Aunt Kate would have accepted help until she became so ill that the only choices she had left were to accept help from Welfare or from Linn. Linn's eyes misted as she recalled the pitiful pride that had kept Kate Marshall going, trying valiantly but in vain to provide for herself and Penny.

Linn's well-formed lips curved into a gentle smile and her eyes glowed with pride. *But now look at Aunt Kate and Penny,* she exulted silently. Penny was the picture of vibrant youth and Aunt Kate, while still thin, was well and full of life. Kate had taken some classes and was now proudly earning a good salary in the Whitebird branch of Clay's business.

Clay had insisted that Aunt Kate work only three half-days a week on this trip. He felt she had been consistently overdoing since returning to work. Kate had agreed and was enjoying her free time immensely.

Linn had reached her room while musing over all that had happened. Entering, she kicked off her shoes. She was satisfyingly tired and decided that a quick shower would be refreshing before lunch. A few minutes later, refreshed from her shower, Linn opened the door of the bathroom and crossed the deep-piled carpet in her bare feet.

Flicking on the light switch, she rolled back the sliding door to the spacious walk-in closet — and screamed in terror!

Coiled about an upright clothes rod support, not a foot from her face, was five feet of living, rippling, emerald-green snake!

2

The large head of the serpent, its round eyes unblinking in the bright light and its wicked, forked tongue flicking, leaned away from the post toward Linn's head.

In terror-stricken panic, Linn screamed shrilly again and backed away. Her heart thudded heavily against her ribs. Fear made her mouth as dry as cotton.

The reptile dropped silently to the floor and began slithering into the room after her. Fearfully, Linn took several quick, backward steps away from the snake and stumbled over the shoes she had kicked off earlier. She tried to regain her balance but her limbs seemed numbed from panic and fear. She fell sideways, striking her head on a heavy antique desk as she went down.

Momentarily stunned, and with a throbbing pain in the right side of her head, Linn struggled to rise. *I — must — get — away — from — that — horrid — thing!*

Trying to focus her eyes against the raging pain in her head, she looked around wildly. There was no sign of the snake now — perhaps she had frightened him when she fell. *But he couldn't have gone far,* her mind reasoned fearfully. *He must be lurking somewhere in the room. I must get up and out of here!*

Holding her head with both hands to ease the blinding pain, she rose shakily to her feet and lurched to the door. Staggering out into the hall, she leaned against the wall while her wide, terrified eyes searched for the huge snake, fearful that he had come out into the hall. But he was nowhere to be seen.

That hideous snake must still be hidden in my room, she thought. *I must keep him there!* Trembling, she slid along the wall and drew the door closed.

Suddenly Linn heard excited voices and running footsteps, and was quickly surrounded by anxious faces. Aunt Kate, Penny and Mrs. Benholt, the housekeeper, were all talking at once, wanting to know what was wrong. Still shaking badly, Linn finally got out the words, "There-there's a s-snake in m-my room!"

Unbelief registered in Mrs. Benholt's face. "There couldn't be!" she declared.

Penny's eyes were wide with concern for Linn, but suddenly she grabbed her mother's arm. "Alfred's boa constrictor!"

Neither Linn nor Kate knew what she was talking about and only stared blankly at Penny.

Penny shook her mother's arm, "Alfred has a pet snake! A big, green boa constrictor! He told me about it. It must have gotten out of Alfred's room!"

Mrs. Benholt was shaking her head. "It couldn't be! I've given Alfred strict orders that if that snake ever gets out of his room, out goes the snake for good! He's had it for two years and it has never been out of his room!"

"There's a first time for everything," declared Kate. "Let's investigate."

At her mother's instruction, Penny dashed into a nearby room and brought a chair for Linn who was beginning to calm down somewhat but was still pale and shaken. Penny stood by Linn's chair with her arm around her while Mrs. Benholt and Kate opened the bedroom door. Cautiously stepping into the room, Mrs. Benholt swept the room with her eyes. Advancing further into the room, she called, "I don't see a thing."

Linn had recovered sufficiently from her

fright to move to the open doorway. Kate had followed Mrs. Benholt into the room. Moving to the French doors she drew back the heavy drapes, flooding the room with light. There was nothing visible.

"Are you sure there was something in your room?" the housekeeper asked, disbelief showing plainly on her angular face.

The experience was still so vivid in Linn's mind that she could almost see again the large weaving head with its glittering eyes, and the rippling green body of the snake. She shuddered.

"Positive!" she declared.

Penny had entered the room behind Linn and was slowly circling it, looking behind the furniture and gingerly lifting the floor-length window drapes. She knelt down and looked under the huge waterbed. Scrambling to her feet, she called excitedly, "There's something under the bed!"

Mrs. Benholt clumsily got down on her knees and looked under the bed. "Well, I'll be!" she exclaimed.

Linn felt her heart quiver but made no move to look under the bed. She asked breathlessly, "Is he under there?"

Mrs. Benholt didn't respond, but got to her feet with a grim expression on her face. Marching over to the intercom on the wall, she punched a button and spoke brusquely, "Alfred, are you down there?" There was an affirmative answer almost immediately. "Alfred," his mother's voice sounded very angry, "come up here to Mrs. Randolph's room and collect your snake!"

As Mrs. Benholt turned away from the speaker, Josie appeared in the doorway. "Is anything wrong?" she asked.

"Alfred's snake got out and somehow ended up in Mrs. Randolph's room. He gave her quite a scare," the housekeeper explained tersely. "Alfred will be grounded for not keeping his pet shut in his room," she finished heatedly. "And I just may follow through with my threat to make him get rid of that snake. It gives me the creeps anyway."

Linn was about to protest against the sterner punishment when Josie spoke up with a quizzical expression on her face. "That isn't like Alfred. He's always careful to shut his snake in its cage when he's away even briefly. Alfred is very responsible with his pets."

Mrs. Benholt ignored Josie. Linn had observed in the short while they had been at Moonshell that the housekeeper scarcely ever seemed to take any notice of her shy, gentle daughter. Alfred she usually babied, and Joe she obviously respected, but Josie she ignored unless her services were required.

Suddenly Josie let out a distressed cry. "Mrs. Randolph, you're hurt! I'll get an ice pack." And she left the room on the run.

Linn gingerly put her hand to the right side of her head. She had forgotten about her throbbing head in the excitement of searching for the snake. A large lump had swelled out from her hairline. Her fingers came away sticky with blood oozing from a small cut there.

Kate gently pushed Linn into a chair. Penny hovered about her like a little mother hen, her face pale and anxious, until Linn gave her a jaunty grin and assured her it wasn't anything but a little bump on the head. Penny appeared somewhat relieved but still looked uneasy.

Within a few minutes Josie was back with an ice pack. She examined the cut gently before laying it on the large protrusion. "Mrs. Randolph, you really should see a doctor. There is always the danger of a concussion, you know."

Linn's head was still throbbing but the pain was definitely diminishing. "You're almost a doctor, Josie," Linn smiled. "You'll do just fine."

Josie smiled back shyly, "Then as your doctor, I recommend that you go to the emergency room in Rockport and have a real doctor examine you. They have facilities there in case there is a problem."

When Linn demurred, Josie urged her to at least let someone know if she began to get drowsy or felt strange in any way.

Alfred had followed Josie into the room and was trying to coax the boa constrictor from his place of concealment under the low waterbed. His mother stood nearby. Although she said nothing, her countenance was stern and forbidding. Alfred kept glancing nervously in her direction.

Joe appeared in the doorway just as his younger brother managed to get his hand on the snake. With a gleeful, "Got him!" Alfred slid the boa out from under the bed and held him up triumphantly. Almost instantly its tail coiled itself around Alfred's arm. The large head with its unblinking round eyes and black darting tongue curved up over Alfred's shoulder and around his neck to appear on the other side of his head.

Linn, still clutching the ice pack to the side of her head, stood up and hastily backed away. Penny stood her ground but her green eyes had grown wide and wary.

"Won't he bite?" Penny asked in fascinated awe.

Alfred tapped the snake lightly under the chin and it opened its mouth to reveal rows of fearsome looking teeth. "He could," Alfred admitted, "but he's tame as a cat. Come on and pet him. He won't hurt you."

At first, Penny touched the snake's smooth green scales hesitantly, but with Alfred encouraging her, she was soon stroking him quite fearlessly. The reptile seemed to like the touch of their hands.

"I'm sure sorry King scared you so bad, Mrs. Randolph, but he never meant to hurt you." Alfred's voice was contrite.

Linn drew a long shuddering sigh. "It's okay, Alfred. I wish I didn't have this crazy phobia about snakes, but I just do! Maybe in time I'll get over it. He is pretty," she added charitably.

And he was — if you could call a snake pretty. Primarily a brilliant emerald green, he had large white markings on his back while his underside was bright yellow.

"King is an Emerald Tree Boa," Alfred said proudly. "Their natural home is in the trees of South America, but they can swim well, too. They're the swiftest of the boas and have a tail that is real flexible so they can hang on to branches of trees. Don't you want to pet him?" Alfred coaxed.

But Linn could not be persuaded to touch the snake. "I hope you won't let him go wandering about the house again," Linn admonished.

Alfred's face suddenly went very serious. "I'm positive I locked King in his cage this morning when I went out to help Joe in the flower beds."

His brother Joe snorted, "Now, Alfred, you know that no one fools with that reptile but you! So if he got out, you just didn't lock the cage tightly!"

Alfred's face took on an adamant, defiant expression. "I know that I carefully locked that cage before I went outdoors! And it was wide open when I checked after Mom called me."

"Then you need to fix the lock so he can't get it open!" his brother declared angrily.

"It's impossible for King to get the door open by himself the way it's made!" Alfred argued heatedly. "And I know it was locked when I left this —"

"That will be enough, young man!" Mrs. Benholt broke in. "Stop arguing with your brother. Take that snake out of here and lock him up good this time!"

Alfred looked as if he were about to explode but, instead, he ducked his head and started out of the room. His face set in angry defiant lines, he muttered what sounded like, "I know what I know!"

The pain in Linn's head had subsided and the fear had drained away. Her mind was alert and sharp again. Like a flash, a question dropped into her consciousness: How had that large boa constrictor gotten past the closed bedroom door and into her closet which also had a closed door?

"Just a minute, Alfred," Linn said. She lowered the ice pack. "Are you sure that snake was in your room when you left it — about an hour ago, I believe you said?"

Plainly it was important to Alfred to clear himself and he answered unhesitatingly, "I'm positive King was there about an hour ago and that I locked him into his cage before I left." He shot a stubborn glance at his brother.

Joe opened his mouth to speak but Josie spoke first, "I'll vouch for the fact that the snake was in Alfred's room an hour ago. I went to his room to tell him that Joe needed his help in the weeding. He had King out of his cage and was handling him.

But why is it important?"

Instead of answering, Linn asked Josie a question of her own, "Have you been in my room in the last hour or so?"

Josie thought for a moment, "No, I haven't." Linn turned to Mrs. Benholt, "Have you been in this room in the past hour or so?"

Joe, a scowl darkening his face, spoke before his mother could answer, "Are you accusing us of something, Mrs. Randolph?"

"No, of course not," Linn said soothingly. "But I have just had a disturbing thought and I need some answers."

"I don't mind answering," the housekeeper said. "I've been in the kitchen all morning doing my baking."

"And the part-time maids aren't working today, are they?" Linn queried.

"That's right," Mrs. Benholt confirmed.

"The question bothering me is: How did Alfred's snake get into my room? Both the closet door and the bedroom door were closed and no one had been in there while I was out. So how could King get locked into my closet?"

Joe's face was now a thunderhead. "You are accusing one of us of deliberately putting that snake in your room to frighten you!"

Linn put up a placating hand and began to deny that she was accusing anyone of anything, when Mrs. Benholt, looking as grim-faced as her son, said, "Maybe your aunt or Penny were in your room and the snake crawled in undetected."

"I was in town all morning. I just arrived a few minutes ago," Kate said. "And, of course, Penny was with you, Linn. But why is it so important to you how he got in?" Kate asked quizzically.

Linn spoke apologetically. "I just thought it was strange that the bedroom and closet doors were both closed when I left — and when I returned — but Alfred's snake had somehow gotten inside. I hadn't really meant to make an issue of it. I was just thinking out loud. I can't think of anyone who would want to put a snake in my closet to frighten me, though. Let's forget the whole thing."

3

By evening Linn felt fine. There was still some swelling and soreness, but the lump on the side of her head was much improved.

Clay, Eric and Linn had planned a steak cookout for that evening. Young pastor Stanley Haskins and his wife, Ellen, from the small church on the edge of Rockport which Clay, Linn, Kate and Penny had attended twice, were invited as special guests. Clay and Linn had had little opportunity to really get to know the Benholts and had also invited the whole Benholt family to the cookout.

Mrs. Benholt had insisted on helping prepare the meal, but Clay had been adamant in his refusal to let her. This was to be their hardworking housekeeper's and her family's night "out." He and Eric were to be the exclusive cooks.

As Eric and Clay skillfully set to work, Linn watched the two close friends with pleasure. Both men were tall, Eric topping Clay's lanky six foot frame by a couple of inches. Clay was definitely the more handsome one of the pair, with his thatch of burnished, reddish-brown hair, hazel eyes, square jaw and strong high forehead. Eric's straight, darkish-blond hair, clear-cut features and teasing blue eyes were not outstanding, but he had a certain charm and wittiness about him that set him apart in any crowd. With much kidding around and camaraderie, they prepared the meal with an unhurried efficiency.

Grilled steaks were Clay's and Eric's specialty and they cooked them to each individual's preference. There was also corn on the cob — covered with butter and wrapped in foil before being placed on the enormous outdoor grill; baked potatoes — baked in a microwave oven sitting on a nearby picnic table — and an enormous fresh green salad served with a choice of dressings. Buttery, cinnamony tart-sweet apples, baked over the coals, put the finishing touch to the barbecue.

When the last person regretfully pushed away from the table, unable to eat another bite, Eric took off his large chef's apron with a flourish and took up a ukulele. With an exaggerated bow he said grandly, "You have all partaken of my sumptuous feast so now you must pay the penalty. You must listen to me sing!" And he launched into a nonsense song of several decades ago.

Eric had a collection of records from the 1940s and 1950s, and at any excuse he would sing them; most he knew from memory. His pleasant baritone belting out the words of "The Thing" in a doleful voice soon had everyone laughing and completely relaxed. Clay added his bass during the chorus.

Linn couldn't carry a tune but she always thoroughly enjoyed these impromptu sing-a-longs that Eric, a born comic, directed so well. She noticed that even painfully shy Josie was singing — so softly that the words were not audible to Linn sitting nearby — but singing, nevertheless. Josie's dark eyes were glowing and one small foot was tapping to the rousing beat.

Linn noticed with pleasure how pretty Josie looked. She had fixed her hair and it lay in soft dark curls about her slim face. Color highlighted her cheekbones; her well-shaped lips were parted in a half-smile, and her sparkling eyes showed her absorption in the singing.

Stanley and Ellen Haskins quickly joined in the spirited singing when Eric asked if they would sing. They harmonized on the beautiful old hymn, "Safe in the Arms of God." In the hush that fell over the group while they were singing, Linn felt as if she were in church. The star-strewn sky overhead seemed the ceiling of a vast cathedral.

Eric invited everyone to contribute something to the night's entertainment.

Linn and Aunt Kate declined. "No talent," they laughingly declared.

But Penny quoted a long poem she had memorized for literature class and received cheers. Alfred produced a battered harmonica and played a slow, sentimental tune.

Linn observed that when Alfred was applauded, his eyes quickly sought out Penny's face for her approval. *That boy is certainly smitten with Penny!* Linn thought to herself.

Mrs. Benholt, Joe and Josie all declined to sing or recite when called on, so Eric promptly filled in the gap.

"Everybody help me, if you know this song!" Clay immediately joined in. Suddenly another voice, a pure, bell-like feminine voice, rose softly on the warm night air. Faint at first, it gained volume as it blended with the male voices, harmonizing perfectly. Linn turned to see whose it was.

Caught up in the magic of the music, shy Josie had forgotten herself and was singing in joyous abandonment.

As she glanced back toward Eric and Clay, Linn's eyes passed over Joe. His dark brown eyebrows were drawn together in a frown and his jaw was set in an angry line as he watched Josie sing. Linn's heart gave a lurch of dismay. Why was Joe angry with his twin sister? His stormy eyes never left her face as she sang. When the song ended, Linn saw Joe make a move to rise, but Eric's voice stopped him. Obviously he had seen the look, too.

"Hey, Joe," Eric's voice was jovial, "that sister of yours can really sing!" He turned to Josie. "Sing one by yourself now."

In the sudden attention Josie stammered, "I — I couldn't."

Joe spoke quickly, "Josephine is too bashful to sing by herself. You'll have to excuse her."

But Eric ignored Joe. "Say, lady," he addressed Josie, "our voices go together like honey and butter. Please join me again." His voice took on a teasing note as he fell down on one knee and spoke in a pleading voice, "You'll break my heart if you say no!"

At his affected, woebegone expression

and comical stance, Josie began to smile and then to laugh. "Most of the songs I know well are old ballads that Mother used to sing to us when we were kids," she said apologetically.

Eric grinned his most winning smile — the one which had captured the attention of more then one fair maiden. "Great! I'll see if I can catch the melody and harmonize with you." He began to strum the ukulele.

Josie began to sing timidly but the sound of her voice rising sweetly and clearly seemed to give her confidence. Soon she was singing strongly and well. Linn was entranced by the simple, almost monotonous tune. It was sad, but fascinating, nevertheless. It told the true story of the hurricane which had slammed into the Gulf of Mexico and had driven a wall of water into the city of Galveston, Texas in September of 1900, creating terror and destruction. Over six thousand persons were killed.

When the last sweet note had died away, Ellen spoke quickly, "Josie, I would love to have you and Eric in our church choir. I've already snagged Clay."

Joe answered before Josie had time to speak, "We have our own church to go to!

But thanks anyway," he stated stiffly, the frown still furrowing his brow. He stood up. "It's time we went to bed. We've got to work tomorrow. Mother? Josie?" It was a command.

Mrs. Benholt got to her feet instantly and briefly expressed her thanks to her hosts and hostess. Alfred whispered something to her but she shook her head. Looking crestfallen, Alfred followed his mother up the path after a muttered "Thank you" to the crowd and a subdued "Good night" to Penny.

Joe stood waiting for Josie, looking stern and unbending. She made a reluctant move to rise and Eric moved swiftly to her.

"The evening's young yet, Josie. We've just found out our voices harmonize well together. Stay a little while longer so we can sing some more."

Josie looked at Eric and then at her scowling brother. Slowly she came to her feet. "I'm sorry, Eric. I would really like to stay but I don't think I should," she said softly. The animation had disappeared from her face. "Good night all, and thanks." She turned and preceded her brother toward their own quarters. Eric stood and watched them go.

Stanley Haskins rose to his feet "We left

our two little ones with a babysitter so perhaps we had better be moving on, too. We had a —"

"Can you beat that!" exclaimed Eric, still staring after the now vanished Benholt twins and unaware of interrupting the pastor. "He orders her around like she was three years old — and she obeys as meek as a lamb!"

"Joe has probably always dominated her," Clay stated placatingly.

"That's a good illustration of how Satan dominates people," Pastor Haskins said thoughtfully. "They serve him all of their lives and don't realize they could be free to really live."

"But this is real!" Eric spewed. "A grown woman letting her brother boss her around like that!"

"Follow me around awhile and see the ruined lives I'm called upon to try to salvage and I think you will be convinced Satan is real, too, and very busy," the pastor said dryly.

Eric's face turned a bright shade of pink. "I'm sorry, pastor. I — I guess you know more about that sort of thing than I do. But I don't mess around with the devil and he doesn't bother me."

"I beg to differ with you," Stanley said.

"Those who don't serve God are manipulated by Satan like puppets on a string."

"I don't profess to be a Christian but the devil doesn't manipulate me. I do what I want to do!" Eric said emphatically.

"There's no middle ground," Stanley said earnestly. "There are only two sides and we are either on one side or the other. That old serpent is wise. He doesn't tempt everyone in the same way. Some would never rob a bank or commit murder or even be immoral no matter what, so he uses different tactics on them. He may tell them they are so good they don't need to be forgiven. Then he leads them right down that pleasant path to their eternal destruction."

"And you're telling me I'm on the wrong side," Eric stated.

"You don't have to be," the pastor said gently. "It's your choice. Your grandfather, Adam, sold you out long ago. You and I were automatically on the wrong side the day we were born and it takes definite action on our part to change that."

Eric dropped his eyes uncomfortably, but he didn't turn away.

"It's a simple step to be on God's side," Stanley continued. "Just talk to God and acknowledge your need of forgiveness. Accept God's Son, Jesus, into your life as Savior and Lord. If you'd like, it would be my pleasure to pray with you right now."

The pastor's wife, Linn, Clay, Kate and Penny had withdrawn discreetly to one side and were conversing quietly together. Linn and Clay had prayed for two years for Eric. He attended church with them occasionally, and several times they had felt he was on the edge of committing his life to God, but he had always backed away.

For a long poignant moment, Eric stood very still. Then he seemed to shake himself and expelled his breath with a regretful sigh. "I plan to make that choice sometime, but I guess I'm just not quite ready." He turned away and began to gather up the paper plates and cups, feeding them to the dying fire piece by piece.

4

Linn awoke the next morning with a vague, unhappy feeling. Rocking gently in the king-size waterbed, she tried to determine the cause. She had kissed Clay good-bye as he went out the door before daylight. He and Eric had had an early appointment in Corpus Christi with a contractor. She had gone back to bed.

Then she recalled the conversation she and Clay had had as they strolled along the beach last night, hand in hand. The rest of the family had gone to the house shortly after the Haskinses had left. When Clay had suggested a moonlight stroll, she knew he wanted to talk and the deserted beach was the perfect setting for an intimate chat.

The moon shining over the wide expanse of silvery-black water, the soft murmur and slap of the gently rolling waves, and the soft call of waterfowl had seemed to cast an enchanted spell over the night.

But the beauty and quiet had not been able to completely dispel the keen disappointment each felt at Eric's failure to commit himself to Christ.

"I guess I have a fear that Eric will harden his heart to the gospel until he no longer feels the tug of God," Clay confided to Linn. "We have seen him at the point of decision so many times in the past two years and he always puts it off."

"I know, that's what I have been afraid of, too. But fear is not faith, so let's just claim him for God and leave him in God's hands," Linn said. So there in the moonlight they had turned their faces to the sky and committed Eric to God.

Suddenly Linn knew why she felt this vaguely unhappy feeling. She was allowing the disappointment of the evening before to cloud her mind again!

She closed her eyes and prayed, "Father, I thank you that you heard Clay and me relinquish Eric into your hands last night. I refuse to worry about him anymore but am trusting in your promises."

Linn could feel the worry drain away. Reveling in the luxury of lying in bed, she let her eyes rove about the spacious bedroom. Moonshell was the epitome of comfort and beauty. The early morning sunlight slanted into the room through the lacy panels covering the French doors that opened onto the east porch.

Before retiring the night before, Linn had drawn back the heavy wine drapes so she could awaken to the splendor of the sun splashed about, as it was now. The rich walnut, antique furniture shimmered in the sunlight and the burgundy designs in the plush grey carpet glowed. The huge waterbed was the only concession to modernity and its headboard was crafted in the same ornate design and from the same lustrous wood as the antiques.

Linn sprang from bed and padded in bare feet to the French doors, swinging them wide. The huge, fiery sun appeared to be sitting in the middle of its own immense, rolling waterbed which seemed to be spread with a glorious gold and crimson comforter.

Linn laughed aloud at her fanciful thoughts.

A psalm she had read the morning before crossed her mind. Taking her Bible from the stand beside her bed, she opened it and read, "The heavens declare the glory of God. . . . In them He has set a tabernacle for the sun, which is like a bridegroom coming out of his chamber."

Linn loved the Psalms. They seemed so often to express her innermost feelings. She read them often and had committed a good many to memory.

Finishing her morning devotions, she dressed and went down the hall toward the stairs. Absorbed in her thoughts, she almost collided with Josie who was coming out the door of a room on her left.

Josie apologized but Linn laughed and assured her that she wasn't at fault.

"I had such a good time at the barbecue last night," Josie confided. "Those delicious steaks, the singing — everything was such fun!"

"I'm glad," Linn said, smiling into the dark shy eyes. "Eric is quite a ham, isn't he? There's never a dull moment when he's around."

A faint blush rose in Josie's cheeks. "That's the first time I ever sang for anyone but my own family." She laughed. "I don't know how I ever got the courage to try but Eric — Eric just seemed to draw the song right out of me." She blushed again.

Dismay rose in Linn's heart. Was Josie falling for Eric? If she was, she was probably asking for a broken heart. Eric's special charm and wit drew girls like honey does a bear. Many an attractive young lady had tried to get a matrimonial noose on Eric but not one had succeeded thus far. Linn didn't think Eric purposely led girls on. He just liked the company of the fairer sex, and knew how to entertain them and make them feel special.

Parting from Josie, Linn stuck her head in Penny's and Kate's rooms and inquired if they were about ready for breakfast before going on downstairs.

Josie was setting breakfast on a small, white, decorative table on the shady south porch when she got there. It overlooked a panorama of rolling, silver waves, and, closer to hand, a flower garden that contained nearly every color and variety of blossom imaginable. The aroma of the gorgeous blooms and the melodious hum of the bees and insects were almost as inviting to Linn's aesthetic soul as the delicious meal that Josie was laying out on the table.

Kate and Penny arrived shortly and while they ate, Penny carried on a steady chatter about shell collecting — and Alfred.

"Alfred's going to be a marine biologist, Linn. But he already knows lots and lots about shells and things in the ocean." Penny's bright eyes grew wide with admiration. "He could name every one of the shells in my pail!"

Studious Alfred Benholt had most assuredly made a hit with Penny, Linn mused silently. Penny was an avid reader, interested in everything, so an intellectual would intrigue her.

"Alfred should only be in the ninth grade but because he was so advanced, he skipped second grade. He's a sophomore in high school," Penny finished in an awed voice.

Murmuring an acknowledgment of Alfred's abilities, Linn steered the conversation into other channels. Aunt Kate was home today so Linn grabbed the opportunity to spend more time with her. Kate possessed just the right combination of humor and seriousness, plus an ability to demonstrate her love.

They decided to combine a little sightseeing with some needed shopping. Alfred, who seemed to be Penny's shadow, stood around looking unashamedly hopeful of being invited on their excursion. Linn, wanting her aunt and Penny to herself, would have called a merry, "We'll see you later, Alfred," but Penny came to his rescue.

"Is it okay if Alfred comes, Mother?

Linn? He knows all the best places to visit."

"It's fine with me, dear," Kate replied merrily. Linn, swallowing her disappointment at the intrusion, added, "Of course, if it's all right with his mother."

Mrs. Benholt beamed when her son asked permission to go. "Alfred isn't strong," she confided to Linn. That seemed to be her favorite phrase when she spoke of her wiry younger son. "That's why I don't require a lot of work from him. He's asthmatic, you know."

Linn had observed that Mrs. Benholt was a tireless, hard worker and it seemed to Linn that she worked her older two, Joe and Josie, unmercifully. During the summer they worked as maid and gardener-maintenance man to make enough money to help carry them through their school year at college. Even with the scholarships each had earned, there were still clothes to buy and their old rattletrap car to keep in repair.

In spite of Alfred's presence, Linn had a delightful morning. Alfred was not only an apt guide but he did, indeed, have a great deal of knowledge in his shaggy brown head which he dispensed in an unoffensive manner when it was needed. He was not cocky or arrogant and before the morning was over, Linn found that she liked Alfred.

That evening Clay and Eric took Linn, Kate and Penny out to dinner and it was about nine o'clock when they returned. As they were making their way into the house from the side entrance, they saw Joe and Josie headed for the Benholt apartment.

Eric called to Josie, "Hi, Josie, how about coming out on the porch and singing for a little while?"

Color rose in Josie's cheeks and she replied a little breathlessly, "I'd love to. Let me go change my dress."

"You're pretty just the way you are," Eric said, "but you might need a sweater. It's a little cool out tonight."

Remembering how Josie's brother had acted the night before, Linn glanced at Joe now. His jaw was set in a firm line of disapproval. Josie had not looked at her brother, but darted away and quickly returned with a bright sweater.

"I'll not be late," she told Joe. She seemed in a hurry to get away.

"See that you aren't," Joe said curtly. "Mother has a big day lined out for tomorrow."

Josie didn't answer, but hurried to join Eric at the door. He had already brought his ukulele from a downstairs cabinet where he kept it within easy reach. Smiling down at Josie, Eric pushed the door open and let her precede him out onto the south porch.

As Linn saw the glow in Josie's eyes and the animation in her face, she once again felt strong concern.

Please, Eric, she pleaded in her heart, *don't break that sweet child's* heart. Linn was confident that Josie, as shy as she was and kept under Joe's domination, had never had the opportunity to date much and perhaps not at all.

Eric invited the others to join them, but Clay said he was tired and wanted to retire early. Kate, Penny and Linn decided to follow his example.

But long after Linn heard Clay's steady, even breathing she was still awake. She kept seeing Josie's shining face and sparkling eyes. *You're as bad as Joe,* she chided herself. *We all seem to feel Josie has to be taken care of like a child. But she's twenty-three years old.* Just the same, Linn prayed earnestly that God would protect Josie from having her heart broken.

5

The next morning the carpenter delivered the shell display case Linn had ordered. She had it placed in the large conservatory. The many beautiful flowers used throughout the house were grown here. There was a large, shallow double sink and a concrete floor so they could wash, clean and dry their shells before they were placed in the display case.

Alfred had taught them to prepare their few live specimens by a slow cooling, freezing and thawing process which minimized the possibility of fine cracks in the shell.

The case, which was bolted to a matching waist-high stand, was made from walnut, sanded and shellacked to bring out the natural beauty of the wood. Shatterproof glass covered a honeycomb of open boxes. The different sizes were designed to house Penny's and Linn's growing shell collection. Inside, the bottom and sides were covered with pale green velvet. They planned to take the display case home with them at the end of the summer as a lasting reminder of the glorious, sun-filled hours spent at Moonshell.

Now that the case had finally arrived, Penny and Linn took time to arrange the shells which they had already prepared. They found that Alfred was almost a walking library on marine life and had several good books on sea life, as well. He was eager to help, so the three of them spent an enjoyable morning working on labeling and sorting their shells.

Linn was astonished and Penny was enthralled with the fascinating stories Alfred related while they worked. Linn typed the names of the shells as they were placed in the display case, including other information such as the scientific name, class and where the shell had been found. Most of the shells Alfred named for them, but for the ones he didn't know or was unsure of, they pored over his informative books.

When they were all arranged to their satisfaction, the three stood back and admired them. They represented the work of many hours of walking, searching and cleaning. The delicate colors and breathtaking sculpture of the shells were set off to perfection by the pale green background. There were periwinkles, whelks, one conch, a pair of butterfly wings, an Atlantic oyster drill, two dogwinkles, limpets, helmet shells, cowry and three moon shells.

The Atlantic moon shell was three inches long and a smooth, tannish-grey; the inch-long brown moon shell was a lustrous brown. But of the three moon shells, Linn's favorite was the perfect, inch-long, glossy white, globular milky moon shell. This was the one the mansion they were living in resembled. They put just one of a kind in the case, keeping all the extra or imperfect shells in a plastic basket, hoping to find better ones.

That afternoon, with Clay at the tiller of the Moonshell yacht, they all went deep-sea fishing. Linn delighted in the sport and was rewarded with two large ocean trout and a flounder. Clay brought in a redfish but Eric caught the prize of the day — a very large king mackerel. Penny and her shadow, Alfred, didn't fish but seemed to have a good time just being with each other.

Late in the afternoon, everyone except Eric and Clay went ashore on an island to search for shells. Penny let out a whoop of joy when she found an unusually pretty moon shell. About two inches long, it was blue-white with a brown top. Alfred's quickly consulted shell book called it a shark-eye. Later in the day Kate discovered another blue-white moon shell but with chestnut brown spiral bars and spots.

That night Linn and Penny laid the two new moon shells in the case. They were jubilant! They now had five different moon shells — the most of any one variety.

Two lazy, uneventful days passed. But Sunday evening Josie went with the family and Eric to church. Joe, working outside, saw her about to leave with them and called her. Linn watched as Josie listened to what he had to say, and then came on to the car, leaving Joe staring after them with angry eyes and set jaw.

The next morning Linn woke with a feeling of joy. The pastor's wife had again invited Eric and Josie to join the choir. Josie had accepted without hesitation. Linn knew this would not set well with Joe. But, Eric and Josie had also been very attentive during Pastor Haskin's sermon, and on the way home Josie had asked several questions about the personal experience of inviting Christ into one's life as Savior and Lord. She was confused — but open for instruction. Eric had been quiet but thoughtful.

A soft tap on the door broke Linn's reverie. She hurried into a housecoat and went to answer it Josie stood there.

"I saw Mr. Randolph, Eric and your aunt leave for the office," Josie said. "Could I talk to you for a moment?"

"Certainly," Linn answered. "Come on in and sit down."

Josie nervously looked both ways down the hall before stepping quickly into the room. She seemed ill at ease and said she only had a minute so she couldn't sit down. She came right to the point.

"I don't usually talk about personal matters to anyone outside of my own family but I just have to talk to someone! Joe and Mother are very angry with me about going to your church and joining the choir. They told me — well, Joe did, and Mother agreed — that I'm being disloyal to our church and to the family. Joe forbade me to go." Her voice broke and she turned away, going to stand at the open French doors.

After a moment she regained control of herself and continued. "I have always done what Joe told me to do. Always!" She turned back to face Linn. "I'm sure this seems strange to you, and to the others, too. I could see it in your faces the other night."

"Josie, it really isn't our business if —"

"I want to explain. Joe was always stronger and bigger than I was. He always bossed me, but he also protected me and took care of me. Mother has been the housekeeper here since before we were born and was very busy. She had to work because Daddy was a shrimper and his work was seasonal. He drowned when we were ten.

"When Daddy died Mother considered Joe the head of the house. She never liked girls much and pretty well ignored me. Joe has always seemed older than me. He decided we should both be doctors and I never thought of disagreeing."

Josie looked down at her clasping and unclasping hands. "He could always talk me into anything or, if that didn't work, he would bully me into it. He said we shouldn't waste our time on dating until after we had our degrees and I agreed to that, too. Besides, we have never had time for anything, it seems, but work."

Josie raised her troubled dark eyes, "I have always idolized Joe with his quick mind and self-reliance. I didn't really mind his dominating me until a few months ago when I decided I wanted to be a pediatrician. But Joe insists we both be surgical doctors so we can work together as a team."

"Your rebellion has not just begun, then," Linn said.

"No, I have been trying for some time to get through to him that I don't want to be a surgeon. But he doesn't take me seriously."

"Can't you just go ahead and make your plans? Then he will know you mean business."

"You don't know Joe! He's a bulldozer. He'll just go ahead and sign me up for the same classes he is taking!"

Josie sighed, "It would be much easier for me if I took the classes he takes, I know. He has a much quicker mind than I have and he has been such a help to me in my studies. I doubt that I could have kept up the high grades we both have if we hadn't studied together. He coached me when I had trouble understanding something."

"A mind that doesn't work quite as quickly does not necessarily mean one that is not as sharp," Linn said. "A person who takes longer to think something out is usually more thorough. And even if Joe did coach you, you still made those good grades yourself, so you have the ability to learn whatever you want to learn — and without his help, if necessary."

"It scares me to death to think of trying to do anything without him, but I have about come to the conclusion that I must try. He is now trying to direct my whole life, even to my soul's final destiny!" she said bitterly.

"I don't want to cause a rift between you," Linn said, "but I'm certain you can make it. And if you take God into your life, you will have His help, too."

Suddenly Josie stepped forward and gave Linn a quick, impulsive hug. "Thanks for encouraging me," she said gratefully. With a shy smile she went quickly away.

"Well," Linn said aloud as she walked out onto the balcony, "there is rebellion in the camp."

But she knew Josie would not have it easy. Both mother and son were arrayed against her and their strong characters might overpower Josie's more gentle and sensitive spirit.

She prayed as she leaned on the balustrade that God would draw Josie to Himself and meet the spiritual needs of the rest of the family, giving them family unity.

Linn had just gone back into her room and picked up her Bible when Penny burst in without even knocking.

"Linn, our moon shells are gone! Every one of them!"

"Gone! But who would have taken them?" Linn asked incredulously.

Penny grabbed Linn by the hand and began to pull her toward the door. "I don't know, but come and see for yourself. Only the moon shells are missing."

"Let me get into some presentable clothes first," Linn insisted.

But a few minutes later, when she examined their display box, Linn saw that Penny was right. The cards she had typed were still in their places but the shells were gone.

"Maybe Alfred took them out for some reason," Linn said.

But when Penny and Linn found him outdoors, helping Joe with some painting, he was as shocked as they were. Joe also expressed surprise.

"They aren't valuable," Joe said, "so I can't see any reason someone would steal them. Besides, I haven't seen anyone hanging around here."

They went in to breakfast When Josie

54

and Mrs. Benholt were informed of the disappearance of all five moon shells, they appeared as mystified as Linn and Penny.

"Moonshell's beach is private and posted against trespassers," Mrs. Benholt said, "so it is unlikely that someone came in and stole them. Is there a possibility that Mr. Randolph, Mr. Ford or your aunt took them?"

Linn didn't think it was likely but agreed they would have to be content with waiting until they came home to find out for sure.

But they didn't have to wait. A couple of hours later when Linn and Penny arrived back home from a trip to the library, Linn found the moon shells lying on her bedside stand on top of a sheet of red construction paper! Scrawled on the paper with a black felt-tip pen were the crudely printed words:

THE BOA WAS YOUR ONLY WARN-ING. MOONSHELL DOES NOT WANT YOU HERE! REMEMBER, MOON SHELLS ARE NOT SWEET AND GENTLE. THEY ARE VICIOUS KILLERS WHO BORE HOLES IN THEIR VICTIMS AND DEVOUR THEM!

6

Linn stared incredulously at the note. Was this a practical joke of some kind? She read the few words over again. Fear, like an icy wind, blew over her, penetrating every fiber of her being, setting her stomach to quivering and her heart to hammering crazily.

Whoever wrote this note also put that snake in my closet! It wasn't an accident! Linn's thoughts raced. Whoever it was must also have ready access to the whole house because these five moon shells had come from downstairs in the conservatory and now they were here in her room! *But who in this house would want to frighten me?* If this was a practical joke it wasn't amusing! It was sick!

Suddenly Linn was aware of a faint scent of perfume — a familiar scent, but one which she couldn't place. Picking up the note, she sniffed. The paper was definitely the source of the perfume odor. She strove to recall who wore this exotic and titillating scent. There was a good chance that the person who wore this perfume had written the note. But try as she would, she could not trace the memory.

Suddenly Linn had a frightening thought. *The person who left this note might still be in the room!* She felt like fleeing but a Scripture she had read that morning sprang into her mind: "The angel of the Lord encamps all around those who fear Him, and delivers them."

"Dear God," Linn said softly aloud, "if your angel is in this room with me, I don't have to be afraid." She could feel peace calm her fear. Gradually the spasms in her stomach subsided; her heartbeat returned to normal, and her panic was stilled. As soon as she was calm again, Linn thoroughly searched the two rooms and bath that made up their suite but found no trace of an intruder.

She decided to hide the note so she could show it to Clay when he returned. Slipping the note and shells underneath her clothes in a bureau drawer for safekeeping, she closed and locked the French doors from the inside before leaving the room and then locked the doors leading into the hall.

This time, instead of going down the hall to the main stairs which led to the first floor, she located the smaller back stairs and descended to the first floor and then on down to the boathouse beneath.

A canal of thick, steel-reinforced concrete had been built between the huge old mansion and the bay. The canal ran into the boathouse which was connected to the house and porch. The yacht as well as a small sailing boat and a couple of motorboats were housed in it.

A jetty of pilings and concrete ran into the bay on the south side of the canal to protect it and the small dock. Large slabs of concrete and rock were piled on each side of the concrete ramp extending into the ocean.

Linn came out into the boat garage and walked along beside the water until she came to a door. She took the stairs leading up to the ground level. A sidewalk ran along the top of the short canal with a strong mesh safety fence between it and the canal. Following the sidewalk brought her quickly to the beach, where she turned to her right and walked the short distance to the jetty.

A soft breeze, tasting of salt, touched her face and fanned her fair hair. She walked out on the jetty and listened to the raucous calls of the soaring, squabbling gulls. She liked the methodical sound the waves made as they rushed in upon the large rocks.

Two bright-eyed terns, perched on one large rock, suddenly scrambled forward. A large wave had come in and then retreated, leaving small silvery minnows wriggling upon the wet surface of the rock. Before the waves returned, the terns had devoured most of the stranded minnows.

Linn walked to the end of the jetty and wished she had brought fishing tackle. She hadn't tried the fishing from the jetty but surmised it would be good. She sat down on the hard, cool concrete, resting her feet on a tilted slab of concrete. She could see minnows darting about in the shallow water above a submerged boulder.

Linn had put her mind in neutral but now in this peaceful setting, she allowed the implications of the strange note to surface.

As she reviewed the note in her mind, it sounded more like a genuine warning to her — or possibly to the whole Randolph family and Eric, since they were all newcomers here. The warning to get out of Moonshell could only mean there was real danger here. That the note was meant to frighten them, she was certain.

Linn had made no secret of the fact that she thought Moonshell was a beautiful, romantic sounding name for the magnificent old home, and that its charm and elegance had been all and more than she had envisioned. Frighteningly, the writer of the note apparently knew this.

MOON SHELLS ARE NOT SWEET AND GENTLE. THEY ARE VICIOUS KILLERS WHO BORE HOLES IN THEIR VICTIMS AND DEVOUR THEM!

A chill went down her spine. Linn knew nothing about the habits of moon shells but determined to change that when she returned to the house. Alfred's books should tell her something about them.

A sudden thought struck her. Alfred! He knew all about shells and marine life. Could he have written the note? If so, why? She could think of no reason. He seemed to like her.

"Why would he wish to frighten me?" Linn said aloud.

Suddenly she had another thought. Maybe someone was warning her of impending danger to help her, not to frighten her.

Far out in the water, Linn absently noticed a silver and green boat. Her eyes were upon it now as she weighed the words of the note. Abruptly, her mind registered what she was seeing.

A fisherman was standing in the boat — or was he a fisherman? Although he was quite far out she could still see him. What had caught her attention was the man was not holding a fishing pole but appeared, instead, to be holding binoculars. He was watching Moonshell!

Now that her attention was directly on the boat, she was sure she had noticed a silver and green boat bobbing in the waves offshore several times in the three weeks they had been at Moonshell. Was something going on at Moonshell? Were they under surveillance by the police, or worse yet, by criminals?

Giving herself a shake, Linn told herself out loud, "My, my! You have certainly got an imagination!"

She looked out at the small boat again. The man was seated again and he seemed to be holding a fishing pole. *I'm just getting jumpy,* she thought. *Now I expect mysterious happenings to pop up everywhere. The man probably just laid his pole down and stood up to stretch. He might not have been using binoculars at all. It was too far to see distinctly.*

Glancing at her watch, she saw it was twelve thirty-five. Clay had said they planned to be home at one today to eat lunch with Linn and Penny.

I want to take a look at Alfred's shell book before Clay gets home, she decided, and moved up the gentle slope toward the house. She knew Alfred had left it in the conservatory on a shelf so they could refer to it as they selected shells for their display case.

As she neared the open door of the conservatory, her rubber-soled shoes made no noise on the smooth concrete sidewalk. She paused in the doorway. Alfred was bending over the display case. When she spoke his name, he jumped.

"Y-you startled me," Alfred stammered.

Linn thought he looked extremely uncomfortable. A wild question shot through her mind as she moved toward him and the display case. Had he taken the five moon shells and was now taking others? But even as the thought entered her mind she scoffed at it. Alfred knew all the best places to hunt shells. There was no reason for him to take shells from their meager, beginner's collection.

"Alfred, I would like to use your shell book, if I may."

"Sure, Mrs. Randolph, it's right over there on that shelf; I'll get it."

Alfred seemed extremely ill at ease, Linn thought as she moved forward to the shell display case. She glanced down and her green eyes widened with shock. Ensconced in their pale green velvet beds were the five moon shells which thirty minutes before had been hidden in her bureau drawer with the warning note!

"They're back!" Linn exclaimed. "Alfred," her voice was stern as she turned to face the boy. "Did you take these shells and place them in my room with a threatening note?"

"No, ma'am!" Alfred said, clearly dismayed, "I just now discovered they were back here in the case. Honest, I didn't take them."

"I found these shells and a strange note in my room earlier today but didn't tell anyone," Linn said. "I hid them and the note so I could show Clay when he got home. I haven't been out of my room over thirty minutes and yet someone has been back in my room — and I locked the doors! — found the shells and put them back in the case. What's going on here, Alfred?"

Looking extremely distressed, Alfred backed away. "I told you the truth. I don't know anything about the shells disappearing or being back here in the case. I got here just before you and I was trying to figure out how they got back into the case, too."

"And you didn't write that note?"

"No, ma'am!"

"I'm sorry that I jumped all over you, Alfred, but when I saw you bending over the case and the shells were back I just jumped to the conclusion that you —"

"It's okay." Alfred's face split in his shy grin. Then the grin slowly faded. "What did the note in your room say?"

"The note! Let's go see if it's gone, too." Linn turned and dashed from the room with Alfred right behind her.

Racing upstairs they found the bedroom doors still securely locked, but when Linn checked the chest of drawers — the note was gone! Somehow she had suspected it would be. Her bureau drawer had not been disturbed. Everything was the way she had left it, except the note — and shells — were gone.

"What did the note say?" Alfred asked for the second time as Linn stared at her open drawer.

Linn thought a second. "I can't re-

64

member the exact words of the first two lines. But the last two lines said, 'Moon shells are not sweet and gentle. They are vicious killers who bore holes in their victims and devour them!' "

Alfred frowned. "Everybody who knows anything about sea life knows that a moon shell, as well as some other sea snails, captures a clam or other bivalve with its unusually large foot and holds it while it drills into the shell and eats it. Why would someone tell you that?"

Linn shivered, "So it is true! I was going to check your shell book to see if it was." She shuddered again. "I have no idea why someone would tell me that. I was hoping you might know. Is something strange going on around here?"

A flicker of fear or some other strong emotion crossed Alfred's face. Whatever it was, it was gone so quickly that Linn wasn't sure it had been there. But she thought his denial come too quickly and too vehemently.

"Of course not! What could be going on here?"

At that moment, Josie appeared in the doorway. "I was working down the hall and saw you two come in here. Is there a problem?"

Linn told her briefly about finding the five missing moon shells in her room lying on her dresser with the crudely printed note. "I locked the doors and went down to the beach for a little while. When I came back, the shells were back in the display case and the note is gone from my room."

Josie looked worried, "I'm as mystified as you both are. What do you make of the note?"

"I think someone is either trying to frighten us or warn us of some danger," Linn said.

"Nothing like this has ever happened before," Josie said. "I don't understand it."

After Josie and Alfred went downstairs, Linn laid down and tried to rest. But she was too upset about this newest occurrence to rest. Getting up, she went downstairs and out onto the porch to watch for Clay.

Since he wasn't in sight, she stepped off the porch and walked toward a colorful gazebo which was screened by shrubs, trees and gorgeous lavender bougainvillea. As she neared the gazebo, though, she heard voices and stopped. Hearing a soft low voice and not wishing to eavesdrop, Linn turned to leave. Then Joe's words caught her ear.

"You seem to have aligned yourself with them against your own family so if that's the way you want it, then that's the way it will be!"

"Joe, what has gotten into you! We have always been so close. There aren't two sides here with me on the side of the enemy."

"Aren't there? What about all the plans we made together. You can't tell me you thought this up all by yourself. You don't even want to be a surgeon now and suddenly you don't like the church you've attended all your life!"

"Joe, I have been trying to tell you for months that I have strong feelings about being a pediatrician instead of a surgeon. Remember, it wasn't I who decided for both of us that we would be surgeons!" Josie's voice had risen, too.

"I know what's best for both of us! If I hadn't helped you, you could never have gotten so far and don't you forget it! I'm not blond-headed and blue-eyed but. . . ."

"Leave Eric out of this! I like him and. . . ."

"And you're making a complete fool out of yourself — hanging on his every word, drooling over him like a sick calf! You make me sick!"

67

Josie was crying now. "It isn't wrong for me to like Eric. You make me sound like a — a bad girl."

Joe's voice suddenly softened, "Josie, you think I'm cruel, but why do you think Eric is making a play for you? You're no more to him than our little flirtatious maid, Cindy. Do you honestly think Eric Ford is interested in you for yourself?

"He and the Randolphs are loaded with money. He's an eligible bachelor and can have the cream of the crop. The poor Benholts who have to struggle and slave to get through medical school are not the cream of the crop! Face it, Josie!"

Linn had been so horrified at what she was hearing that she forgot she was eavesdropping on a private conversation. Joe was manipulating Josie as skillfully as a puppeteer his marionettes. Without even thinking of what she was doing, she strode the few steps to the gazebo entrance and stood in the doorway. Josie was huddled in the swing sobbing.

Linn's eyes sparked green fire, "Joe Benholt, how dare you talk that way about your sister or Eric. Josie is a lovely, intelligent girl and it isn't strange that a young man would notice her. And Eric is a fine man who works hard for his pay and he has

68

no unsavory designs on your sister."

When Linn appeared, Joe was apparently struck speechless. Josie simply stared at Linn with shocked, tear-wet eyes.

Anger flamed in Joe's eyes as he said stiffly, "Mrs. Randolph! I'm surprised you would eavesdrop on our private conversation. We are in your employ and are subject to your orders, but in our private lives I will brook no interference!"

Joe reached out a strong hand and gripped Josie's arm. "Come, Sis, we've got to get back to work."

Josie seemed about to pull away, then casting a look of appeal at Linn, she meekly went with her brother.

7

Mixed emotions surged through Linn's heart as she watched Joe and Josie go. She felt sympathy for Josie, indignation toward Joe, and anger at herself for letting her temper get out of control. Blowing up at Joe would most certainly not help Josie's cause. To the contrary, it could conceivably make matters much worse for her.

Joe apparently felt that Eric and the Randolphs were turning Josie away from her family. He probably had to blame someone besides himself because if he blamed himself he would have to admit that he was a tyrant as far as Josie was concerned.

I may have made an enemy, she thought, *and Joe might be a formidable enemy.*

Hearing Clay's car coming up the driveway, she went to meet him. She decided to not mention the note or her recent dissension with Joe immediately. That could come later, after lunch.

Josie and Mrs. Benholt served lunch on the southeast porch. Penny announced almost as soon as they were seated that the moon shells were missing but Linn told her they were now back in the case. That satisfied Penny, but Clay gave Linn a level look that she knew meant he wanted to hear what was going on later.

Josie was pouring tall, ice filled glasses of tea when Eric asked, "Josie, could you get away this afternoon for a bit of sailing? There's a gentle breeze — just right for a smooth ride." When she hesitated, he continued persuasively, "We could sail down the coast to The Gull's Nest, have dinner and then sail back in the moonlight."

Josie's soft dark eyes sparkled but she said regretfully, "I would love to, but Mother has me scheduled to wash all the windows and it will take all afternoon."

"No problem," Eric declared. "With me helping, we can be through in two hours. I'm the best window washer on the block!"

Before Josie could compose a suitable answer, Mrs. Benholt appeared with a tray of food.

Eric turned his charm on her, "Mrs. Benholt, I would like to request the company of your lovely daughter for an afternoon of sailing and dinner out this evening."

Mrs. Benholt was clearly astonished at the invitation but quickly recovered. "I'm sorry, Mr. Ford," she apologized, "but I just can't spare Josie this afternoon. The windows must be washed."

"With my expert help, we can be through in two or three hours."

"Mr. Ford! I couldn't allow you to wash . . . !"

"I insist! And I promise we won't leave till every window in the place is spanking clean!" Not waiting for any more objections, he turned to Josie, who was standing stock-still, the pitcher still in her hand. "As soon as I gobble some lunch and change to my window-washing duds, I'll meet you back down here."

Before her mother could make further protest, Josie agreed somewhat breathlessly.

True to his word, Eric proved an excellent window washer. He took the outside and Josie the inside. Eric wisecracked and teased Josie as they worked and before either realized it, the windows were shining.

At three o'clock Eric piloted the sailboat from the boathouse. Josie was dressed in white slacks and a red and white silky blouse which set off her short, lustrous dark curls. Eric's straight blond hair was topped by a captain's cap, and he looked quite sharp in casual white slacks and a blue and white striped knit shirt.

Linn was standing on the upstairs porch outside her room when the yacht, with Eric at the wheel, moved out of the boat-house and down the short channel toward the open bay. The couple saw Linn and waved good-bye.

They certainly are a stunning couple, Linn mused, turning her thoughts heavenward.

"*Dear God,*" she prayed earnestly, "*wrap your arms about them and bring them both to a saving knowledge of Christ.*"

Later that afternoon as they were resting, Linn told Clay about the five shells disappearing, then reappearing in her room with the scrawled message on red construction paper. As she related how the note had vanished, and the shells had been removed from the dresser drawer where she had hidden them, Clay's lips tightened but he said nothing until she had finished her story.

"You had locked all the doors and they were still securely locked, but the note and shells were gone?"

"Yes."

Clay's voice was grim. "The first thing

73

I'm going to do is have the locks changed on our doors."

Clay and Linn occupied two large rooms joined together by a luxurious bathroom on one side of a short passageway with an extra closet on the other side. One room served as a bedroom and the other a study, complete with a couch which made into a bed. Clay sometimes used it if he worked late so he wouldn't disturb Linn.

They were sitting in the comfortably furnished study now. Clay reached for the phone and phone book. He called a locksmith and arranged for him to come immediately to replace the locks on not only their doors but also the locks on Kate's, Penny's and Eric's rooms. Since he didn't know who was doing the mischief, Clay was taking no chances.

Suddenly Linn remembered, "Clay, I just recalled something else. That note had a faint smell of perfume — very distinctive — an exotic sort of scent. I know I've smelled it before but I can't think where."

"I'm afraid perfume wouldn't be much to go on," Clay said. "So many wear the same kind."

"I suppose so," Linn agreed, "but there is something about that perfume scent that keeps nagging at me, like it would be a real clue if I could only nail down who wears it. Oh, well," she sighed, "perhaps I'll remember later."

Linn was silent for a moment, then glanced at Clay who seemed lost in his own thoughts. "I don't like to think it, but whoever is trying to frighten me — or us — most likely works right here at Moonshell, one of the Benholts, or possibly one of the two day maids. Unless, of course, someone is sneaking into our room from the outside."

"I'm afraid that about covers it," Clay said gloomily.

"Perhaps new locks will put a stop to this," Linn said hopefully.

"If there's much more of this, I'm in favor of sending you and Kate and Penny back home to Grey Oaks," Clay said decisively.

Linn's face fell. "Surely it won't come to that! I love Idaho and Grey Oaks but Moonshell has been a good change, and we are enjoying the ocean so much. Besides, I don't like the sound of 'sending Linn, Kate and Penny home.' I would miss you terribly!"

"It will be a last resort," Clay assured her. "But that note sure sounded like a threat! I don't even like the idea of leaving you alone anymore. I'll alert Joe to be on the lookout for prowlers."

Suddenly Linn remembered Joe and Josie's argument in the gazebo and told him about it. "I'm afraid I owe Joe an apology," Linn said. "I still think he is a dictator, but I had no right to eavesdrop or interfere. What do you think? Should I apologize?"

Clay suddenly grinned, "I can remember how it used to be. Green fire flashing from your eyes and your words scorching the ground for a mile around! It's a fearsome sight and sound!"

Linn made a face at him. "I'm glad God has changed me and I don't usually do that anymore. I'm so ashamed when I lose my temper. And I did today. Should I apologize?"

"It wouldn't hurt," Clay said seriously, "but frankly I doubt that Joe will accept it. I liked that young man so much at first. I would never have imagined him to be so overbearing with his family and to have such a hair-trigger temper."

Clay was right. When Linn sought Joe out later that afternoon and apologized for listening to their conversation and interfering, he told her stiffly that it was okay. But Linn could see that no warmth or forgiveness reached his eyes.

And when Joe came into the house to see what a locksmith was doing there, Clay informed him briefly about his reasons for having new locks installed. Joe's eyes mirrored instant hostility. He stated brusquely, "So you think one of us is planning to harm one of you."

Clay could be just as plain of speech. "No, I really don't think so, but I must take precautionary measures. I would appreciate it, too, if you would keep an eye out for anyone who doesn't belong here."

Joe promised to do so but stated that he had seen no one thus far.

When Clay mentioned prowlers, Linn recalled the silver and green boat she had seen earlier in the bay. She went swiftly to the porch to see if it was still there, but the only boat there now was a small sailing craft. She didn't mention to anyone that she had thought at first someone might be spying on Moonshell through binoculars.

8

Sometime in the night Linn suddenly awoke. She listened intently, wondering what had awakened her. The only sound was Clay's even breathing. She slipped from bed carefully so as not to disturb him and went to the bathroom. The luminous digital clock gave the time as 2:37.

Linn reentered the bedroom. She still heard no strange sounds, but she felt that something had awakened her. Padding to the French doors, through which a dim light was filtering, she pushed aside the filmy curtain and stared out into the night.

Clouds obscured much of the sky but she could see vague outlines of objects. Was that a movement in the canal? She couldn't tell. Noiselessly, she slid the bolt on the door and crept out onto the porch, keeping low. Cautiously, she looked over the edge of the banister surrounding the porch.

At first she could detect no movement

and then she heard a hushed bumping sound almost directly below the porch. Straining to see, she held rigidly still. At first she wasn't sure and then suddenly some of the clouds shifted to let a portion of moonlight through. Indistinctly, she saw a small dark boat slipping along the canal bank toward the bay, keeping in the shadows.

She more sensed than saw the mysterious boat slip away into the darkness of the open bay waters. *Did I really see a boat?* she questioned silently. She waited for several moments, feeling the dampness of the night seep through her housecoat. But she neither saw nor heard anything more.

An eerie feeling prickled down her backbone. She crept softly back to bed and lay wide awake for a long time. Had she really seen a boat in their private canal?

I think I did, she decided. *But if I did, it's gone now. Should I tell Clay what I saw?* She decided against it since she wasn't even positive she had seen anything. He was on the verge of sending her back home anyway and she didn't want to go.

The next morning, the first thing she did was go down the back stairs to the boathouse and look around. As she stepped down onto the concrete dock, she met Alfred who seemed startled to see her. Feeling somehow that she had to explain her presence, Linn gave him what she hoped was a casual smile and told him she was just looking around. Suddenly, though, she was aware that Alfred also seemed a bit sheepish about being there. Had he heard something last night, too, and come down to investigate?

"Alfred, did you hear something last night?"

His denial was quick. "No, ma'am. Why?"

"I thought I might have, but I'm not sure." She looked about and saw that all the boats were there. "Anyway, the boats are all here so I guess everything's okay. I'd better get up to breakfast."

At breakfast, though, Linn noticed that Josie was not helping to serve as she usually did. Linn inquired if Josie was sick but Mrs. Benholt said she was just busy elsewhere and didn't elaborate. But when Mrs. Benholt served lunch without Josie's help, Linn began to suspect that Josie was being kept away from them.

Linn knew that Eric and Josie had come in at about nine last night, looking happy and relaxed. Eric had gone upstairs for his ukulele and Josie had stayed, joining Clay,

Linn, Kate and Penny in singing several songs before she reluctantly took her leave. With shining eyes she had thanked Eric for a wonderful time.

Eric, Clay and Kate were busy at the office that afternoon and didn't come home for lunch so Linn decided to do some exploring. Penny was engrossed in a mystery story she had borrowed from the library yesterday, so Linn was on her own. She had gone up to the tower room once with the others but now determined to explore it more fully since she was alone.

Stairs off the second story balcony led to the tower's circular porch. From there a steep, narrow set of metal steps ascended to the widow's walk perched like a flat, cocky hat on top of the tower, forming its roof. A sturdy railing encircled the small platform.

When Linn came out onto the widow's walk, with binoculars strung about her neck, she looked about and exhaled rapturously. The view was spectacular!

Linn reveled in the panorama as she slowly followed the railing around the walk. She could see far beyond the border of land that separated their bay from the Gulf of Mexico. A huge oceangoing ship anchored offshore looked like a child's toy boat. In their own bay, the white-crested, blue-green waves rolling onto the pale tan sand looked like an artist's seascape painting.

Linn lifted the binoculars to her eyes. Swinging herself slowly around, she studied the landscape and then the sea. She could see tiny figures on the deck of the huge ship. Lowering the glasses to scan their bay, she could see two small boats, one close and the other near the strip of land that hemmed in their bay.

Moving the binoculars over the nearer boat, Linn felt her heart begin to beat a little faster. The small craft was silver and green! As she watched, the man in the boat rose up onto his knees, lifted binoculars to his eyes and slowly moved them over Moonshell.

Linn darted quickly to the stairs and down to the tower room, not wishing to be seen. She kept out of sight until she saw him lower the binoculars, sit down and take up his fishing rod again. Then she moved out into the open and studied the man through her own glasses.

The man was redheaded with a full, dark red beard. He wore a limp fishing hat and a grey and black flannel shirt. To the casual observer, he appeared to be no more than a casual fisherman.

But Moonshell was being watched! Linn was sure of it now as her pulse began to race. Something was going on at Moonshell! There had to be! But what? Was it something illegal? And was someone trying to frighten the Randolphs away from Moonshell because of what they might stumble onto?

Linn suddenly remembered the dark, silent boat in their private canal last night. She hadn't imagined it! Had Alfred heard it or seen it, too? If so, why had he denied it so quickly? Was Alfred involved in something shady? It seemed preposterous! He was only fifteen-years-old!

Joe, perhaps. No, if Joe was involved in something questionable, he would never have been instrumental in getting them here. Or would he? Maybe he needed someone to front for him. Linn's thoughts raced with possibilities.

The house and grounds were immense. With the men and Kate away a great deal, and she and Penny out on the beach, sightseeing or shopping much of the time, all kinds of things could be going on in and around Moonshell and they would be unaware of it. A chill swept over her as she felt goose bumps crawl over her skin.

Could the whole Benholt family be involved in something dishonest? She really couldn't imagine gentle-as-a-dove Josie as anything but the epitome of lawfulness — but then she seemed to have little to say about anything in their family.

Linn shook her head. It was hard to believe any of the Benholts would do anything illegal. Joe was domineering within his own family, but he exuded reliability. But one could never tell. Medical school was expensive and if one needed money badly enough . . . and there were two of them to put through school plus Alfred coming on.

Linn knew that the Benholts had both gone through four years of college on full scholarships. But Josie had said they would have to pay their own way for the next three years. Even with working every summer, three more years of medical school for both Joe and Josie would be extremely hard to manage, she knew. But it was still difficult to envision the Benholts involved in anything dishonest.

Linn put the binoculars to her eyes again and studied the redheaded man in the boat. Suddenly he began to reel in and soon she saw a flopping silver fish dangling from his line. Removing the fish from the line, he placed it on a stringer that was trailing the boat. The man re-baited the hook and cast out into the water again.

Linn was about to drop her binoculars when suddenly the man laid the rod down and picked up his binoculars. But this time he didn't aim them toward the house. Linn turned her own glasses in the direction he was looking.

Coming along the beach was an older lady with a small shaggy dog on a leash. She was dressed in bermuda shorts and wearing a huge, floppy straw hat. It wasn't often that anyone walked on the beach below Moonshell. It was well-posted against trespassers and a fence ran down to the water's edge. *Probably a tourist,* Linn thought, shrugging. She didn't seem to be bothering anything. Linn would have passed it off but the fisherman never took his glasses from the woman on the beach. So Linn continued to watch them both.

The woman strolled slowly along the water's edge. Occasionally she stooped to pick up a shell or rock. Most she threw away but a couple she stowed in the large straw bag she carried. When she came to the Moonshell boat dock, though, she stopped. Taking a small black object from her bag, she turned toward the house.

It was a camera! The whole scene rang false and Linn felt her mouth go dry as she watched the woman closely. The old lady was taking pictures of Moonshell from every angle. Then, moving rather quickly for an old woman, she walked to the narrow canal and snapped several pictures from different angles of both the house and bay ends of the canal.

The whole episode took probably no more than five minutes. Linn watched as the woman placed the camera back into her bag, turned and walked back the way she had come. While not moving rapidly, she no longer stopped to examine anything.

From her elevated vantage point, Linn saw her go around the fence at the water's edge and then walk rapidly back to the road. A small grey car was parked there. Getting in, the woman drove swiftly away.

Linn swung her binoculars back to the bay. The fisherman had gone back to his fishing but Linn knew he had watched the woman out of sight first.

Excitement, mingled with apprehension and alarm, pulsed through Linn's body. That innocent-looking stroll down Moonshell's beach had not been a wandering tourist. What did all this mean? Moonshell was being spied upon from the bay and now it had been photographed.

Should she tell the Benholts? *No,* Linn decided, *I'll wait till Clay comes home and see what he advises.*

Not wanting to go back downstairs yet, Linn went into the little tower room and poked about in the cupboards. They contained very little except a few paper plates, cups, napkins and some forks. *The tower room must be used for picnicking sometimes,* she thought. She found writing paper and a few envelopes in a box and an electric coffee pot on another shelf. A small, round metal table and four chairs were the only furnishings.

Linn glanced at her watch. Two o'clock. She still had most of the afternoon before her but there seemed nothing more of interest here. She took one last look at the fisherman. He was still fishing at about the same place.

Linn had started down the steps leading to the second floor when she spied a scrap of red paper lying on the second step. She picked it up and her heart missed a beat. It was a piece of red construction paper! The kind of paper the note in her room had been written on!

Excitement beating in her throat, she

carefully searched the floor of the tower porch, the stairs leading down to the second floor and even went back up onto the widow's watch and searched there. She discovered three more tiny bits of red paper. The writing on them had been done with a black felt-tip pen — just like her note.

Obviously the person who had taken that note from Linn's bureau drawer had brought it up here to the tower, or the widow's walk, torn it into tiny bits and tossed them out so the wind would scatter them.

Another chill coursed through Linn. Was the note a threat from a foe or a warning from a friend?

9

As Linn reached the second floor balcony, she heard Penny excitedly calling her name. Seeing Linn, Penny skipped up to her, her eyes looking like two sparkling green stars.

"Linn, look what Alfred gave me!" She lifted a small object suspended from a gold chain about her neck for Linn's inspection.

Looking closely at the little green pendant, Linn saw that it was an exquisitely fashioned, oddly shaped lizard.

"It's beautiful!" Linn said. "When did Alfred give you this?"

"Just now. I got hungry so I went down to the kitchen for an apple. Alfred followed me out and gave it to me. Do you think Mother will let me keep it?" she asked anxiously.

Linn looked at the small object again. "I expect so. If it was expensive, I'm sure she wouldn't. But I doubt that Alfred would have the money to buy an expensive gift."

"I hope I can keep it," sighed Penny. "It's the loveliest thing I ever saw."

Linn thought it was beautifully made also. *Some lovely things can be made with inexpensive materials now,* she reflected. And the chain was pretty, too, intricately woven but a little heavier than the usual chain. She hoped Penny wouldn't be too disappointed if it turned her neck.

When Kate, Clay and Eric returned later that afternoon they, too, duly admired the little lizard pendant. Kate agreed that it couldn't be expensive. She didn't think it would hurt for Penny to keep it.

Clay was the only one who didn't say much about the gift and Linn saw that he kept glancing at it all during dinner. Linn knew something was troubling him.

Linn also observed that Josie did not appear to help serve dinner. She said nothing to the others, but she was almost certain now that Josie was being kept away from them.

Dinner was almost over when suddenly Linn heard Eric call Mrs. Benholt to the table. "Is Josie sick?" he asked.

Mrs. Benholt's eyes slid away from Eric's as she said reluctantly, "She's cleaning cupboards."

Eric wasn't shy. He rose from the table.

"I want to speak to her," he said and walked back toward the pantry. Mrs. Benholt looked upset but followed him into the kitchen. They could hear him call, "Josie!" and a muffled reply.

When Eric returned to the table a few minutes later he looked angry. "There's a conspiracy going on to keep me from seeing Josie," he declared. He lifted his coffee cup and sipped slowly as if to calm himself.

After a moment he said, almost as if he were talking to himself, "I really like that girl. She's intelligent, full of fun — and honest. She's the first girl I ever dated that I felt like I was seeing the real person inside and not a facade."

He paused and looked intently at Clay. "Josie has a certain innocence about her that is so refreshing after all the sophisticated, finishing school girls I've known."

Suddenly Eric laughed, "Say, I may be falling in love." His eyes were twinkling, but Linn's cupid heart began to beat faster. She had never heard him speak about any girl as he had just now about Josie. Men were so unpredictable! She would never have expected Eric to look twice at an unworldly-wise person like Josie.

"I'm taking Josie out for a moonlight

ride in the sailboat tonight, if you aren't using it, Clay."

"And stand in the way of true love? No way! The boat's all yours," Clay answered, grinning.

"And you, dear husband, are taking me for a ride right now," Linn interjected. "You've been promising to take us to see the shrimp boats. Remember?"

"How could I forget, with you reminding me every minute?" Clay said in mock annoyance. "See, Eric, what you can get yourself into? Nag, nag, nag!"

"Seriously," Linn said, "if you are too tired we can do it another day."

"A ride in that powerful motorboat will be just what I need to unwind," Clay assured her. "Would you and Penny like to go, too, Kate?"

Kate looked uncertain. "Clay, you and Linn don't have a lot of time together. You two go on and have a good time."

When Kate refused to listen to either Clay's or Linn's argument that they would love to have them, Penny looked downcast. But her mother promised to take her — and Alfred — to see the water skiing exhibition that evening which cheered her up instantly.

The fleet of assorted shrimp boats was

very interesting to Linn and Clay. They cruised about, viewing them from different sides, and even talked with the captain of one. On the way home, Clay raced the boat to get the feel of its power. Skimming madly over the waves brought a delightful feeling of exhilaration and excitement. The wind whipped at their hair and the salt spray stung their faces.

When they neared home, Clay cut the motor and they sat holding hands, rocking peacefully in the gentle waves on the dock side of the jetty. The sun was very low and the western horizon was aflame. After a few minutes of quiet, Clay spoke, "I'm selfishly glad that we didn't have anyone else along this evening."

"Me, too," replied Linn, "it's so peaceful out here rocking in the waves that it almost puts one to sleep."

Suddenly Linn saw Clay smile broadly. "You wouldn't believe what Eric said to me today, Linn. Our Eric, who has safely escaped many a girl's matrimonial snare, seems to be in the process of losing his heart to a fair maiden."

"What?" Linn asked in astonishment. "You don't mean —"

"Oh, but I do mean. Eric confided to me that he has never felt for any girl what he feels for Josie. He can't seem to get her off his mind and he really isn't trying to. He told me that they can talk for hours and never grow tired of each other's company. When I teased him about being careful or she might snag him, you know what he said?"

"No. Tell me!" Linn urged.

" 'I might not be hard to snag.' "

"You're kidding! Eric really said that?"

"Yes. Isn't that exciting? He said he hadn't ever met anyone like her and their silences were as sweet as their conversations."

"Oh, Clay, I hope it does work out for them. I know Josie likes Eric a lot and I'd hate for him to break her heart."

Suddenly Linn remembered Clay's reaction to the necklace Alfred had given Penny. "Clay, you acted strangely when you saw Penny's pendant. What didn't you like?"

"I'm not sure," Clay said, "but for one thing I don't think that lizard is made of cheap materials. I'm almost certain it's handcrafted jade and the chain is real gold."

Linn gasped. "Are you sure? Where could Alfred get money to buy an expensive gift like that?"

Clay's brow was creased in a frown. "That's part of what troubles me." He paused and searched Linn's face. "I'm not going to say this to anyone but you until I know for certain, but I don't think that piece could be purchased anywhere in a store. Did you notice anything odd about that little lizard?"

"Just that he was oddly shaped. Clay, what do you mean, you don't think that necklace could be bought at any store?"

"That lizard is an iguana."

"Of course! It's like those huge lizards like they have in the zoo! But what if it is an iguana?"

"I guess I'm afraid to say it in case I'm wrong, but I believe that piece of jewelry is from an Indian grave or ruin in Mexico."

"What makes you think that?" asked Linn in amazement.

"Iguanas live in the tropics and just across the Gulf of Mexico from here are the Mexican jungles of the Yucatan. The ruins of the Mayan Indian civilization are scattered throughout the jungles there. It seems logical to me that Penny's necklace could have come from one of those ruins."

Linn could feel her heart beating a tattoo on her rib cage. "B-but, if you're right, how did Alfred get it?"

"I don't know," Clay said grimly, "but don't give even a hint of this to anyone until I have a chance to check it out. I studied archaeology in college, but I'm far from an expert. I want to talk to someone with real expertise in the archaeological field.

"One thing that caught my eye, though, was that neither the pendant nor the chain were perfect. Beautifully done but not perfect. That's a good indication that they were handcrafted."

"Penny will be devastated if she has to give up that necklace," Linn said sadly. "And wouldn't Alfred be in serious trouble if it truly is an art treasure from Mexico?"

"Possibly. But let's not jump to any conclusions until I look into this."

Suddenly Linn reached out and gripped Clay's arm. "The man in the boat! The one watching Moonshell through binoculars!"

At Clay's astonished expression, Linn began to laugh. "I forgot I hadn't told you." So she told Clay all about the fisherman in the boat, the older lady on the beach, and her picture-taking.

When she had finished, Clay sat for awhile, deep in thought. Finally he said, "I'll admit it appears the man in the silver and green boat is watching Moonshell. The picture-taking also looks suspicious, but there could be logical explanations for both. Many people carry binoculars and use them just to see what they can see.

"It's also possible that the lady is just a tourist who wanted some pictures of our very old and beautiful mansion. Perhaps she was afraid she would be run off before she could take them since the area is posted against trespassers."

"Oh, Clay! You can take the mystery out of everything!" Linn said in mock dismay. "Here I was imagining the FBI or the Mafia had us under surveillance, and you puncture my big red balloon with logic!

"Okay. I won't worry. But what are we going to do about Penny's necklace?" Linn asked seriously.

"I'll do a little sleuthing and see if I can come up with a reputable expert on Mayan art. In the meantime, we won't tell Penny about my suspicions until we have something to go on, one way or the other."

That night Linn dreamed. In the dream she was fleeing from a small, dark boat which held dark indistinct figures. She was swimming up the canal toward the boat-house and they were close behind her. Try as she would she could make no headway.

She was straining — straining — straining to swim away from them until her arms were leaden and she was gasping for breath. But the frightening dark boat glided closer and closer and closer. It was almost upon her when she awoke with a start, wet with perspiration and totally exhausted. She was trembling, her stomach was tied in knots, and her mouth was dry and cottony.

Linn raised herself on one shaky elbow and saw with vast relief that she was lying beside Clay in their own comfortable bed. She lay in the semi-darkness, her quivering stomach gradually stilling, and wondered why she had dreamed such a dream. Was she subconsciously worried about the things transpiring at Moonshell?

Suddenly her body went tense again. She heard something! It was a faint, almost inaudible bumping noise — like a boat gently touching the sides of a wall! Swiftly, but carefully Linn slipped out of bed and rushed to the open French doors. Easing out onto the balcony, she peered over the railing, down into the murkiness of the canal.

There was more light tonight. This time Linn saw a small, dark canoe-like boat slipping almost noiselessly toward the boathouse. Linn's extremely keen hearing detected the careful dipping of the oars into the water. The boat was now out of sight. It must be inside the boat garage!

Speeding noiselessly back across the porch into the bedroom, Linn dashed to Clay's side and began shaking him. "Clay! Wake up! Clay!" she whispered urgently. He came groggily awake but was instantly alert when she explained breathlessly about the boat.

He sprang out of bed, pulled on a robe and stuck his bare feet into bedroom slippers. Whispering for Linn to stay in their room, he ran down the hall toward the steep back stairs, flashlight in hand.

Linn stood in the doorway for a minute, watching as Clay disappeared from sight. Unable to contain her excitement, though, and also fearful for Clay, she raced down the hall after him. She could not see his light when she got to the stairs, but she could hear the faint sound of his slippers on the treads. Quietly, she followed him to the first floor. In the dim hall light, she saw that he had begun the descent to the boat-house.

Clay glanced back, spied Linn and waited for her to catch up. "I'm not going to do anything dangerous," he whispered, seeing her anxious face. "I'll just slip down and see who's there and what's going on. Promise me you'll wait here at the top of the stairs."

Linn nodded and Clay quietly descended into the darkness. Dim light filtered in at the end of the steep stairs, so Linn knew a nightlight burned in the boat garage. For several moments all was quiet. Then she heard movement and Clay rejoined Linn on the first floor.

"There was no one there, but I distinctly heard a boat being paddled away. I think I saw the stern of it but I'm not sure. The boat was already out in the canal when I got to the bottom of the stairs. Either they heard us or their business was very brief."

Clay deliberated a moment. "Why was the bar on the boathouse door off? Did someone from inside the house take it down for them? The prowler must have had a key to the door lock or someone unlocked it for them. Leaving that bar off and the door unlocked is just asking for a burglary. I closed and locked the door, and pulled the bar across it before I came back up here." He yawned. "It's three o'clock in the morning, and we can't solve any of this tonight. Let's go back to bed."

Linn accompanied him upstairs, but

sleep was long in coming to her. All the strange happenings were tumbling about in her mind, and only one thing was certain — something was very wrong at Moonshell!

10

When Linn woke the next morning, it was nine o'clock and she realized Clay had slipped away to work without disturbing her. When she went downstairs, Penny was waiting for her in the dining room, curled up in a big chair reading.

"I told Mrs. Benholt I'd wait to eat until you came down. You're a sleepyhead today!" Penny said.

"Sorry about that," Linn said, "but Clay didn't wake me up when he left and I guess I must have been tired."

Penny was wearing the lizard pendant. Linn lifted it and examined it more closely. Clay was right; it wasn't perfect. But that only added to its value, she knew. The iguana was a marvelously fashioned work of art. The chain was made of tiny strands of interwoven gold material.

"I'm going to wear it forever and ever," Penny said dreamily.

Linn wanted to caution her to not get too attached to the exquisite ornament, but knew it wasn't wise. Clay could be wrong and it still might just be a skillfully fashioned, inexpensive copy.

After breakfast, Linn asked Mrs. Benholt if Alfred could go shelling with them to St. Jose Island, the band of land which protected the mainland from the ocean. The permission given, they set off. Alfred handled the small motorboat skillfully, and showed them the best places to look for shells.

They returned a little before noon, tired but triumphant with several perfect new shells to add to their collection. They sorted and cleaned the shells, laying them out to dry. Since it was still a little before lunch time, the three of them strolled down to the beach. Linn and Penny never tired of feeding the voraciously hungry gulls. As soon as one crumb of food was tossed, it seemed the air would be literally teeming with gulls. It was almost frightening as they descended like a cloud, rending the air with their shrill cries.

Happy and rested, they returned to the house for lunch. As Linn entered the hall, Mrs. Benholt called, "Telephone, Mrs. Randolph. It's your husband."

Linn could hear the excitement in Clay's voice. "I have a guest coming for dinner, hon. Could you have Mrs. Benholt fix something especially good? Esteban Molinas is the head architect for the shopping center project but he's more than that! He's a native of a town in the Yucatan peninsula in Mexico!

"While in college he worked summers with teams from the university, excavating some of the Maya Indian ruins. He's quite an authority on Mayan artifacts. He agreed to come over to inspect the necklace. The Mayan culture is his passion so I think we are in for an interesting evening!"

And they were! Esteban proved to be a delightful man with a tiny mustache and average stature but he was large in every other sense. A leading authority in his field, he could speak knowledgeably on many subjects. But, as Clay had stated, his passion was Mayan culture.

During the excellent meal Mrs. Benholt had prepared, Esteban held his audience spellbound with his charming manners, Spanish accent, and stories of the fantastically advanced Maya Indians.

"Almost a thousand years ago Mayas built fabulous cities in the forests and jungles of the Yucatan. One of the most spectacular was Chichen Itza. Spread over more than a three mile radius were palatial homes, a vast stone stadium where games were played, an observatory where Mayas studied the stars, the roofless Temple of a Thousand Columns, and a magnificent pyramid. Much of this has been restored.

"Called El Castillo, which means 'the castle,' the pyramid is an amazing architectural wonder. The temple which crowns the 100-foot-high structure is reached by ninety steep steps. Inside the inner temple," Esteban told them, "is a stone jaguar, painted with red spots and glowing green eyes.

"The Mayas lived in fear of displeasing their many gods and would periodically sacrifice beautiful young women as brides to the rain god, Yum-Chac, to appease him so he would send rain for their crops."

Linn gasped and Penny asked in horror, "You mean they killed the young girls?"

"The priests assured the people that the 'brides' would not die. Who knows? Perhaps they believed that but, of course, the girls were never seen again until their bones were dredged from the ceremonial wells by archaeologists four hundred years later."

"They were thrown in a well to drown?" Kate asked, shuddering.

Esteban smiled his empathy. "Yes, I'm afraid so. The huge, deep natural wells were called cenotes. Some supplied water for the people and others were used as sacrificial wells. The sacrificial cenote at Chichen Itza is oval and about 190 feet across its widest point. There was about a 70-foot-sheer drop to the water and the water was 60 or 70 feet deep.

"The ceremonial procession began at the temple. Clad in beautiful clothes and decorated with flowers, the terrified virgin girl was led by the high priest down the steep stairs of the pyramid to the accompaniment of wailing flutes and pounding drums, and followed by the other priests and the worshipers.

"At the foot of the pyramid, the death procession crossed on a 15-foot-wide causeway, lined with hundreds of feathered serpent images, to the cenote. Prayers were chanted at the altar in front of the well and then the lovely little maiden was hurled to her doom into the dark waters."

His listeners sat in horrified fascination as Esteban finished his story. "After the human sacrifice, rich offerings such as statues, urns, vases, incense and treasures of gold, copper, and jade were hurled down, too."

"How pathetic!" Kate exclaimed. "Such devotion to a god that doesn't even exist! How thankful I am to live in America in the twentieth century and not be expected to give up my daughter as a sacrifice!" She reached over and hugged Penny.

"Yes," Linn said softly, "and the most pathetic part of all is that God doesn't want a dead sacrifice but a live one who can reflect His love to the world."

Esteban looked uncomfortable. He knew much about the gods of the vanished civilization but he knew nothing about One who could make a face glow as Linn's was now. Adroitly he changed the subject.

Clay had explained to Esteban that Penny's necklace had been a gift and she knew nothing of their suspicions that it might be a Mayan artifact. So now Esteban casually addressed Penny.

"That's a very pretty necklace you are wearing. May I see it?"

Penny was delighted at their erudite guest's interest in her treasured gift. She quickly removed it and handed it to Esteban. He studied it carefully, turning it over in his hands. Taking a magnifying glass from his pocket, he examined it minutely.

Turning to Clay, he spoke almost reverently, "There's no doubt. It's genuine gold and jade — and Mayan." Handing the pendant back to Penny, whose puzzled expression was mirrored in Kate's and Eric's faces as well, he said simply, "It is truly beautiful.

"Now I must go, as much as I would like to stay. It has been such a pleasant evening and the food was delicious."

Amid everyone's expressions of how much they had enjoyed his company, he took his leave.

After he had driven away, Eric cast a sly glance at Clay. "So, there was an ulterior motive involved in having Senor Molinas over for dinner?"

Clay grinned. "I'll admit my guilt. He had some interesting things to tell, didn't he?"

Kate spoke wonderingly, "So he thinks Penny's necklace is a Mayan artifact! Not only very old but extremely valuable, I imagine."

Penny looked from one to the other, bewilderment and alarm playing hide-and-seek over her expressive face. "I won't have to give it back, will I?" Her voice quavered and tears trembled in her eyes.

Then, abruptly, gentle, docile Penny astonished everyone by shouting, "I won't give it back! I won't! I won't! Alfred gave it to me and it's m-mine and I intend to keep it!" Bursting into a torrent of tears, she dashed from the room.

Kate followed Penny but returned in a short while, distress written all over her face. "Linn, maybe you can reason with her. She's locked the door and won't let me in. I can hear her crying her heart out."

But Linn had no better success and soon came back downstairs to the others, "This is not like our Penny," she declared. "What can we do?"

"Let's leave her alone for now," Clay suggested. "This was quite a shock. After she's had time to cry herself out, I imagine she'll let someone in to talk." A while later Linn and Kate went to her room, but there was no sound beyond the door.

"Do you suppose she's asleep?" asked Linn.

"I don't know," said Kate, "but I have an extra key. I'll unlock the door and see."

When the door was open, they saw that Penny had fallen asleep with the little iguana clasped to her cheek. Her pillow was wet and her cheeks still bore the stains of her grief. Kate drew a pink sheet up around her daughter's shoulders, then they tiptoed away.

"What are we going to do?" Kate asked Clay, worriedly, a few minutes later. "The government would never allow us to keep it, would they?"

"I don't know," Clay replied. "But until we have time to find out, it certainly won't hurt for Penny to keep it. And tomorrow I must have a talk with Alfred. I hope that boy isn't in a peck of trouble!"

11

The next morning everyone except Penny was down to breakfast early. Kate was still anxious about Penny, who was asleep when Kate came down, but Linn promised to give her special attention today since Kate was needed at the office.

But just as the men and Kate were about to leave the table, Penny surprised everyone by appearing — with tousled hair and still in her robe. Walking slowly over to the table with a very serious demeanor, she cleared her throat and spoke in a misery-laden voice. "I — I'm sorry I acted like a brat last night. If I have t-to give the necklace back I will."

She was standing near her mother and Kate reached out, pulling Penny to her lap without a word. Penny buried her head in her mother's shoulder and wrapped her arms tightly about her as Kate stroked the fair hair.

Clay, Eric and Linn moved outdoors, leaving the two alone. After a few moments, Kate joined them with purse in hand, ready for work.

"I thought for awhile last night that we might have a temperamental teenager on our hands," she said, "but she's still the loving young lady we're used to. Thank the Lord!"

"She's okay now?" Clay asked.

"Naturally she's still hoping to be able to keep the necklace. But she seems reconciled to the fact that she may have to relinquish it."

"I'll talk to Alfred when we get home," Clay said, "and find out how he came by that pendant before we do anything else. In the meantime there shouldn't be any harm in Penny wearing it. I don't think she should wear it away from the house, though. It could be extremely valuable and if it is, it could cause some questions that we aren't prepared to answer yet."

After the men and Kate left for work, Linn returned to the dining room and found Penny listlessly nibbling at some toast and scrambled eggs.

"I left the little lizard in my room," she told Linn. "I decided it's probably too valuable to wear."

Linn protested. "Clay said he sees no reason why you shouldn't wear it, as long as you don't wear it away from the house."

Penny's eyes lighted up. "If Clay thinks it's okay, then that's what I'm going to do! Wear it every minute as long as I can!" She jumped up from the table. "I'll run up and get it and then finish breakfast." She rushed away up the stairs.

Dear Penny, Linn thought. *She is such a sweet child.* She knew that much of the credit for Penny's respectful attitudes went to Kate who was a loving mother but also a firm one. "Dear God, keep her the way she is," she prayed softly.

She heard the sound of Penny's feet coming swiftly down the stairs. She turned with a smile, expecting to see Penny's face radiant with happiness. Instead, tears were running down her cheeks! Running to Linn, who had risen in alarm, Penny flung her arms around her, sobbing almost hysterically.

"Penny, what's wrong?" Linn queried in a shocked voice.

When Penny could talk she gasped out, "It — it's g-gone!"

"What's gone?"

"My necklace! It's gone!"

"Are you sure?" Linn asked. It seemed incredible. Penny had been gone from her room only a very short time. "Come on, let's go up and check again. Surely you just forgot where you put it."

But a thorough search of the room revealed no trace of the jade pendant. Penny assured Linn in a distraught voice that she knew where she had put it. "I slept with it in my hand all night. When I woke up, I laid it carefully in the middle drawer of my bureau, right on top of my blue pajamas."

They took out every garment in all four drawers but the necklace had vanished.

"Go wash your face, Penny. Then we'll talk to everyone at Moonshell and see if we can get to the bottom of this."

Linn felt anger beginning to boil inside her at whoever had stolen the necklace and upset Penny. Suddenly a new thought froze her. Was this just another link in the chain of ominous happenings which were growing more frequent? Was someone trying to scare them away from Moonshell? Had all the incidents been perpetrated by one person or persons or were they random, unrelated acts?

If someone was trying to frighten them away, who was he or she and why? Nothing made sense. Who of the Benholts would want them gone? Clay paid the Benholts' wages, so logically they wouldn't be anxious for them to go. Alfred certainly wouldn't want them to leave. He followed Penny about like a love-starved puppy.

Linn knew the two day maids were working today so she decided to talk to them and the Benholts immediately.

When Penny returned, they marched downstairs. Finding Mrs. Benholt and Josie in the kitchen, she announced a consultation with the Moonshell staff in the dining room as soon as everyone could get there. She sent Josie to call the maids and Mrs. Benholt to summon Joe.

When everyone was assembled, Linn asked them to be seated. She stood at the end of the table with Penny. The two day maids were on her right and Josie, Joe, Alfred and Mrs. Benholt on her left.

Linn came right to the point. "A valuable gold and jade necklace disappeared from Penny's room just a few minutes ago. First of all, I would like to know if anyone has seen the necklace or saw anyone go into Penny's room." She waited, her eyes sweeping the faces of those before her.

She registered the expressions in her mind. Joe looked angry; Josie seemed shocked; the pretty maid, Cindy, appeared nonchalant; Flora, the other maid, stared blankly. Mrs. Benholt was plainly distressed; while Alfred wouldn't meet her gaze and a faint flush rose in his cheeks.

When no one spoke, Linn looked at Cindy, "Have you been in Penny's room to clean this morning?"

"Not me. Maybe Flora did."

"No, ma'am. I ain't been in nobody's room yet. I just got here a few minutes ago. I was just gettin' supplies together to clean," Flora declared.

"Have you been in Penny's room this morning, Josie?" Linn shifted her eyes to Josie.

Before Josie could answer, Joe burst out indignantly, "Are you accusing Josie of stealing that necklace?"

"Of course not," Linn said calmly. "I'm just trying to discover if anyone saw the necklace or saw anyone take it."

Joe subsided sullenly.

Josie looked disturbed but replied quietly, "I haven't been in Penny's room. I've been in the kitchen for the past forty-five minutes, at least."

"I'll vouch for that," Mrs. Benholt added. "I've been in the kitchen the last hour myself."

Alfred saw Linn's eyes upon him and he reddened, blurting out, "I just got up a few minutes ago."

Linn kept her eyes upon him and said gently, "You gave Penny the necklace, Alfred. Would you mind telling me where you got it?"

Alfred swallowed hard and darted glances at first his mother and then Joe. Then he ducked his head and said lamely, "I found it down on the beach."

Joe was staring hard at Alfred. "You gave a necklace to Penny?" he demanded.

Alfred's head came up quickly, his brown eyes shooting sparks behind his dark-rimmed glasses. "Yes, I gave Penny a necklace! Not that it's any of your business!"

"Alfred!" Mrs. Benholt reproved.

Alfred lowered his head sulkily.

Joe's voice took on a threatening edge. "Anything that goes on in this family is my business, including where you got a necklace to give a girl!"

Mrs. Benholt suddenly took the situation in hand. "Boys! We're here to find out what happened to Penny's necklace."

Linn went on as if the brothers had not been almost at each other's throats. "Alfred, you didn't for some reason have to have the necklace back and just. . . ."

She groped for the right word and Joe finished bitterly, "stole it back?"

Linn was instantly on the defensive. "I

didn't say that! If he gave something of real value and had to have it back for some reason, he wouldn't necessarily consider it stealing!"

"If he stole it to begin with, you mean, and was in serious trouble if he didn't get it back," Joe added malignantly.

This was all getting out of hand. Linn wished she had waited for Clay to handle it.

Linn drew a deep breath. "I'm not accusing anyone of anything. I just want to know if anyone knows anything about the necklace or saw anyone strange hanging around."

When no one responded, Linn asked Joe if he had seen anyone loitering around the beach or the house this morning. He stated decisively that he had not.

Realizing that nothing was being accomplished, Linn dismissed everyone back to their duties with her thanks and an admonition to report any strange person, thing, or happening to Clay or herself.

Linn felt drained by her interrogation of the Moonshell staff and decided to go up to the tower to unwind. She urged Penny, who looked very unhappy, to get Kate's binoculars and join her. Penny brightened up a bit and agreed.

So a few minutes later Linn and Penny climbed out onto the widow's walk. After Penny scanned the area for a few minutes with her binoculars, she went back down to the tower room to explore. Linn searched the floor of the walk for more bits of red paper but found nothing.

Penny came out of the tower and trained her glasses on the landscape and beach in front of the house. Linn had her binoculars, too, but for now she just wanted to enjoy the panorama.

She noticed that the little green and silver boat wasn't in the bay today. *Clay was probably right,* she thought, *the fisherman in the boat was probably just a fisherman who carried binoculars along for fun.*

Suddenly, from the narrow tower porch, Penny exclaimed, "Linn, look at the man in the sailboat! He's using binoculars — just like I am!"

Linn swiftly brought her glasses to her eyes. The man not only was using binoculars but he was redheaded and sported a dark red beard! It was the same man from the green and silver motorboat!

Linn watched as the man laid aside his glasses and picked up a fishing pole. He apparently had not seen Linn and Penny — or had he seen them and taken up his fishing rod quickly so they wouldn't know he was watching Moonshell?

Linn was convinced now that the bearded man was watching Moonshell. Prickles of fear danced mockingly along every nerve. What secret danger did Moonshell hide?

12

Linn informed Clay of the disappearance of the necklace as soon as he arrived home that evening. He went immediately to the Benholt apartment to see Alfred in an attempt to learn more about the necklace. But Mrs. Benholt said, with a somewhat reproachful glance at Linn, that Alfred had come down with a severe asthma attack.

"He was terribly upset by the meeting Mrs. Randolph called," she said with veiled accusation in her voice.

After they left Mrs. Benholt, Clay said to Linn, "It might have been better if you hadn't talked to everyone."

Linn was quickly on the defensive. She wished she had waited, too, but it cut her to the quick when Clay was upset with her. "I don't see how you could have found out any more than I did," she said, trying to keep her voice calm.

"Alfred was the one I wanted to talk to

about the necklace. But your little meeting not only didn't help, but it apparently caused Alfred to have this asthma attack and now I can't talk to him," Clay snapped.

Linn was angry now. *Clay is taking out his frustration on me,* she thought. *He is being unfair, but I won't let him needle me into saying something I'll regret.*

She and Clay were both strong-willed and in the early years of their marriage, before they had become Christians, their home had often been a battleground for days on end. This didn't happen often now, but occasionally they still locked horns.

Linn said nothing more to Clay but left him and went to their room to get ready to go out to eat. Clay had made reservations at The Gull's Nest, the seaside restaurant which Eric declared had unrivaled seafood. And although she didn't make an angry retort, she felt vastly abused. *Men!* she thought. *They always think a man can handle anything better than a woman!*

Clay followed her to their bedroom and began to change clothes. "Did you get my tan suit out of the cleaners?" he inquired.

"It's in your closet," Linn said stiffly.

Clay took the suit from the closet and

started for the bathroom. Abruptly he stopped and turned around. "You don't have to pout with me. You know I'm right. You should have let me talk to Alfred like I wanted to."

Linn kept her back to Clay, and stubbornly refused to answer.

She could feel Clay watching her. Then he went into the bathroom. Soon Linn heard the sound of spraying water — and Clay's cheerful whistle. The whistle only irritated Linn more. How could Clay say hateful things to her and then whistle merrily like he hadn't done a thing!

This is going to be some festive evening! she thought. If it wasn't for the others I would just stay home! It occurred to her that she was being as mulish as Clay, but she pushed the thought from her mind. Clay was the one who had started this! Why must she be the one who always made the first move to make up?

Linn finished getting ready quickly and, not waiting for Clay as she usually did, went downstairs to wait until the others were ready. Penny soon joined her, bubbling over with excitement.

Penny loved to eat out in restaurants with "atmosphere" — a word she had picked up recently from a book. She had dressed for the occasion in a becoming new outfit and was even wearing hose and heels — not too high, but as high as Kate would permit.

Linn studiously avoided talking to Clay during the ride down the coast. In fact, she said very little at all. But no one seemed to notice. Eric and Clay were soon talking about the shopping center project, with Kate interjecting a comment now and then. Penny was bouncing up and down and commenting on everything with her usual exuberant interest.

The Gull's Nest occupied the top floor of a luxury resort hotel. The maitre d' led the Randolph party to a table overlooking the bay and the beautifully landscaped gardens surrounding the hotel. A smiling, helpful waiter patiently waited while they studied their menus.

In spite of herself, the loveliness of the scenery, the smiling, solicitous waiter, and the soft dinner music soothed Linn's spirit. Soon she began to feel ashamed of her anger. Suddenly she felt she must let Clay know immediately that she was sorry.

But as she turned toward Clay, she suddenly heard Eric's low whistle and exclamation, "Would you look who's headed our way?"

Linn and the others looked in the direction Eric indicated.

As Linn saw the delicately beautiful young woman approaching, shock caused her to gasp involuntarily. What was Bonnie Leeds doing in Texas? It was the same wealthy, sophisticated socialite whom Clay had been about to marry when he and Linn met. Bonnie had done everything in her power to get Clay back, even after Linn and Clay were married, and she had very nearly succeeded at one point!

Seeing her, Linn suddenly remembered the vow Bonnie had hissed at her once, "If you stand in the way of my marrying Clay, I'll make you sorry you were ever born!"

It had been two years since Linn had seen or heard anything of Bonnie and now here she was, walking gracefully toward them, as petite, beautiful and poised as ever. She was dressed in a simple but elegant cream colored sheath. Bonnie's lustrous black curls were piled on top of her shapely head, her exquisitely shaped lips were curved into a smile. Her melting dark eyes against the creaminess of her perfect complexion were warm and friendly. But as she stopped at their table, Linn noted a certain something, a hardness or callousness about her face that she didn't remember being there when she had last seen her.

"Clay! Eric! And dear Linn! This is such a delightful surprise! Whatever are you doing in Texas?"

Linn couldn't recall later if she even greeted Bonnie, or whether Clay or Eric answered Bonnie, because the scent of her perfume had reached Linn's nostrils. She froze inside, feeling like a cruel, giant hand was squeezing the life from her.

The subtle, exotic scent exuding from Bonnie was the same fragrance that had clung faintly to the threatening note Linn had found in her room with the missing moon shells! That was why the perfume had seemed familiar! It was the expensive, imported perfume that Bonnie always wore.

"Linn, darling," Bonnie's husky, honeyed voice addressing her brought Linn's mind back to her surroundings with a jerk. "I'm having a big party at my suite in the Fountains Hotel tomorrow evening. I would adore having you all attend." Bonnie's gaze had not lingered on Linn, but was concentrated on Eric and Clay.

Linn saw that Clay's hazel eyes were cool. His voice, when he spoke, was formal but polite. "Thank you, but Linn and I have other plans."

Linn thought she detected a slight frostiness in Bonnie's eyes, but it was only for a second and then she laid a slim, jeweled hand on Eric's arm. "But you will come, won't you, Eric? For old time's sake?" Her lips formed a slight, pleading pout.

Eric laughed lightly, obviously pleased. "Sure! Why not? What's the address?"

Bonnie gave him a card, excused herself and left with a little wave of her shapely hand. "I'll see you tomorrow, Eric. 'Bye, all."

Linn watched her gracefully weave her way across the room to a table where a handsome, dark-skinned, dark-haired man sat. Linn watched the man rise as Bonnie approached, his well-chiseled lips below a tiny, trim mustache curved into a charming smile as he drew a chair out for Bonnie.

Linn turned back to Clay and, forgetting that she was angry with him, said excitedly, "Clay, it's Bonnie's perfume that was on that threatening note! As soon as I smelled it I remembered!"

Clay's face registered astonishment but before he could answer, Eric spoke up. "That's absurd, Linn! Why would Bonnie want to leave a note to frighten you — or us — into leaving Moonshell? It just doesn't make sense. And you saw how surprised she was to see us."

"The surprise would have been easy for Bonnie to feign. She is quite an actress when she chooses to be," Clay said thoughtfully. "However, I agree that it doesn't make sense for Bonnie to leave a threatening note at Moonshell. How would she get in for one thing?"

"I don't know how she could get in, but as for purpose, she could still be carrying a grudge against me. Remember, Clay? She promised to make me sorry I was ever born if I kept her from marrying you!"

"But she hasn't even seen you for two years. Surely she doesn't still hold a grudge! People say a lot of crazy things that they don't mean when they're angry," Eric argued.

Suddenly Linn saw that Penny's eyes were big and round with concern. *We'd better drop this conversation right now,* Linn decided.

"Oh well, it has been a long time and you could be right," Linn said lightly, as if it didn't matter to her. Thankfully the waiters arrived at that moment with their food.

Linn was still sorry that she had behaved badly toward Clay, so when she caught his

128

eye, she mouthed the words, "I'm sorry!" He mouthed back "Me, too!" with a warm light in his eyes.

Suddenly everything looked bright again and Linn thoroughly enjoyed the evening. Later when she looked across to Bonnie's table, she saw that they were gone. *I imagine Eric is right,* Linn thought. *Why would Bonnie still carry a grudge after all this time?* Lovely and sought after by half the men she knew, the thought did seem preposterous. Besides, a faint scent of perfume on that note was very poor evidence as to who its writer was.

13

After breakfast the next morning, Linn strolled down to the sequestered gazebo with a book and letter-writing materials. She didn't feel well, an unusual occurrence with her. She had only had orange juice for breakfast because she felt queasy and a little dizzy. Clay had wanted to take her to the doctor but Linn was sure she only had a touch of a stomach flu.

Penny had gone into the city with the men and Kate. Her mother planned to work a couple of hours and then do some shopping for Penny before returning home with the men about one o'clock.

Linn stretched out in the comfortable cushioned swing but even its slight movement made her stomach more uncomfortable, so she moved to a matching cushioned lounge. Stretching out, she tucked a pillow under her head and closed her eyes. She didn't mean to go to sleep but her nausea had subsided and all was quiet about her. The soothing hum of the industrious little gold and brown bees extracting nectar and pollen from the blooms of the honeysuckle vines and the gorgeous scarlet and lavender bougainvillea blossoms lulled her.

A while later she drifted out of a deep sleep into the realization that Joe was working in a flower bed not far away. Drowsily she listened to his low whistling, the sound of earth being turned and the rub, clink and swish of the small garden tools. *I hope he doesn't discover I'm here,* she thought lazily. She just didn't feel up to carrying on even a brief conversation.

Suddenly she was aware that Joe was no longer alone. Josie's soft voice was speaking.

"Joe, you are wrong about Linn. She isn't trying to make trouble for our family. I'm sure she was just trying to find out what happened to Penny's necklace. I wish you wouldn't be so angry about it."

"If you weren't so infatuated with Eric, and the whole kit and caboodle of the Randolphs, you could see they are all just a bunch of troublemakers. Our family always got along fine before they came here." Joe's voice was a growl. "Now you want to change the plans we made when we were kids and be a pediatrician instead of a surgeon!"

"Joe, I have told you repeatedly — even before the Randolphs came — that I didn't want to be a surgeon. You made that decision for both of us. It was never my idea."

Joe went on as if he hadn't heard Josie. "And Alfred is just as bad as you! He never resented my position as head of this family before." His voice rose angrily, "But now he thinks there is nobody in the world but those high and mighty Randolphs!

"He even dared to give that girl a present! She wouldn't give him the time of day if any of her friends were here! He's only the son of their housekeeper," he finished mockingly.

Linn was wide awake long before the discussion between Josie and Joe had gone this far, but she didn't dare show herself lest Joe accuse her again of willful eavesdropping.

Besides that, Joe's words had so upset her that her stomach was again heaving like the waves on the sea. So she lay there, praying she wouldn't embarrass herself by being violently ill or by being discovered.

"I came out here to reason with you," she heard Josie saying now, "but you didn't hear a word I said, so I might as well go.

132

But I still like our employers and think they are some of the finest —"

Joe interrupted savagely, "Of course you do! You even take up for them against your own family!"

"That's not true! How I feel about them has nothing to do with my loyalty to our family." Josie's voice was trembling.

Suddenly Joe's voice went deadly quiet. "If you persist in this foolishness about dating that blond-headed playboy and back out of our plans to be surgeons, there will be no money to pay your tuition this next year!"

There was a shocked gasp from Josie, "You can't do that! Part of the money in the bank account is money I earned!"

"Can't I? My name is the only one on the account."

Josie sounded like she was forcing back tears. "But — but how can you be — so cruel! You know I can't go to school with no money to start."

"I know that. But as the head of the family I must do this to bring you to your senses." Joe's voice was so smug, Linn felt like leaping from her place of concealment and telling him what she thought of him, but she knew this was really none of her business. "You have a choice. It's either give up your dream of being a doctor or give up the Ford guy and become a surgeon like we have always planned."

Joe's voice gentled. "And Josie, it is still tentative, but I'm working on getting a grant that would put us both through the remaining years of medical school."

Josie's voice sounded numb and her words were without expression. "And if I don't, I'm out in the cold."

"That's right. But there's no reason for that to happen. Come on, Josie, we've always been buddies. Let's not let strangers separate us," Joe said persuasively.

Linn heard a choking sound and then footsteps dashing away toward the house. She heard Joe heave a sigh, then a long moment of silence as he obviously watched Josie's rapid departure.

Linn realized her hands were clenched and her nails were biting into her flesh. Tears ran down her own cheeks, wetting the pillow under her head. Poor Josie. What would she do? What could she do?

Linn considered asking Clay if they could give or loan her money, but she doubted that Josie would accept it — especially with Joe feeling about them as he did.

She was vaguely aware that Joe was gathering up his tools. Then she heard his footsteps moving away from the gazebo in the direction of the house. Thankful that he was going away without discovering her, Linn closed her eyes and tried to put the Benholts from her mind.

Lying quietly, she softly quoted the twenty-third psalm. Under its peace-restoring power, her turbulent emotions and rebellious stomach slowly calmed.

Suddenly she thought of Alfred. Linn winced as she remembered the rift between herself and Clay. Thankfully, they had both admitted they were wrong and made up last night.

Before she had known God and His forgiveness, it had been almost impossible for Linn to ask anyone's forgiveness. *Perhaps being forgiven makes the difference,* she thought. *But I should have inquired if Alfred is okay today.* However, in her own misery, she had forgotten he was sick.

After a while she felt better so she sat up and wrote a letter to Clay's mother, Ethel. They had received a letter from her yesterday.

In the first years of Clay and Linn's marriage, the elegant Mrs. Randolph had deeply resented Linn. She had considered wealthy, sophisticated Bonnie Leeds a much more fitting wife for her only son. But since Ethel had become a Christian, she had been kind and thoughtful of Linn.

Linn paused in her writing to think back upon a more marvelous miracle than Mrs. Randolph's conversion. The conversion of Uncle Arthur, Mrs. Randolph's alcoholic brother. Uncle Arthur had been part of Clay's family for years. He had shuffled about in a perpetual alcoholic fog, listless, dull-eyed and pathetic. Everyone reasoned that wine had so muddied his mind that he was beyond help — even from God.

Then Kate and Penny had come to Grey Oaks to live. And Penny with childlike reasoning had not seen Uncle Arthur as hopeless. Pity drew her to the wretched, befuddled derelict. At first he had seemed suspicious of her attentions but soon the skinny little green-eyed child began to get through to his foggy mind. Whenever she came around him, his blurry eyes would brighten and soon it became a normal thing to see Uncle Arthur and Penny absorbed in a simple game of checkers or dominoes. Then Arthur had become gravely ill. The doctor had given him just days to live and the family honored his pleas not to be placed in a nursing home or hospital.

Everyone in the household helped care for the invalid and a nurse was hired, as well, but it was Penny to whom Uncle Arthur seemed to cling. Penny read to him and tried to cheer him in any way she could, staying with him hours at a time until the family began to fear she would fall ill.

One day Penny was reading to him from a Bible story book about heaven, thinking this would cheer him, when suddenly he had reached out a bony hand and clutched Penny's arm.

"I'm scared," he had said. "I'm gonna die and God would never let a dirty old sot like me into his beautiful heaven." He had begun to sob brokenly.

Frightened, as she had never seen him cry before, Penny had run and called for help. Ethel had rushed into the room and gently directed her brother into a prayer of salvation.

Arthur had lived only two more days but the fear had vanished from his eyes. He told everyone who would listen what wonderful things God had done for him. Tears would fill his eyes as he expressed regret that he had nothing to give his Lord except a broken, ruined life and he marveled that God had accepted that. Uncle Arthur had died quietly in his sleep, with a smile on his face.

As Linn mused she felt a surge of joy. There will never be any greater miracle than Uncle Arthur coming to God, she thought. How thankful I am that Penny could see that unlovable, pitiful old man as God saw him.

Linn finished her letter and looked at her watch. It was 10:30. Her stomach seemed almost back to normal so she decided to go back to the house and have some more cold orange juice. Perhaps by lunch time she would be able to eat a meal.

Finding the kitchen empty, Linn poured herself a glass of juice and went to her room. She tried to read but, feeling restless and a little lonesome, she decided to go down to the conservatory. Perhaps Josie would be there tending the flowers. Linn always enjoyed her company.

The conservatory was actually a hot-house where a number of gorgeous plants and flowers flourished. It supplied the house with cut flowers as well as bouquets or potted plants for special friends. Also, Linn regularly supplied their church with flowers from its bounty. Both Linn and Josie were proficient in floral arrangement.

But today Josie wasn't working there, Alfred was. He looked a little pale and was listlessly watering plants. Linn thought he looked alarmed when she entered the room, so she determined to put him at ease.

"Hi, Alfred," she said cheerfully. "I wanted to see you and apologize for upsetting you with that little meeting I called. I guess it appeared that I was picking on you but I didn't mean to. Let's forget the whole thing, shall we?"

Alfred grinned his shy grin and his whole demeanor brightened. When Linn offered to help with the plants, he quickly found her a pair of shears and told her she could trim the dead flowers from the plants. In no time at all, Linn had drawn him into his favorite subject — marine life — and they spent a pleasant thirty minutes talking and working companionably.

Suddenly Alfred stopped working and looked at Linn. "Would you like to see my ferret?" he asked.

"What's a ferret?"

"Wait right here and I'll show you!"

In minutes he was back with a little Siamese cat colored animal. "This is Baby," Alfred said.

The ferret was adorable with her white-whiskered muzzle, raccoon mask, tiny black nose, soft, dark eyes and diminutive white ears. Her long, thin supple body was covered with greyish fur, set off with rich brown markings.

When Alfred put her down she began a systematic search of her new surroundings, poking her sensitive button nose into every nook and cranny. Finished with the room, she came back to rummage in Alfred's pockets. That task completed, the energetic little creature climbed into Alfred's lap and partly turned over on her back.

"Baby wants her belly scratched," Alfred explained as he obliged her by scratching her throat and stomach. The little ferret showed every evidence of being in ecstasy.

"Baby is especially fond of dates," Alfred said. "I'll show you." He darted away and returned shortly with a small package of the gooey fruit.

Baby seized the date that Alfred held out to her and ate it with evident pleasure.

"We must be related," Linn laughed. "I'm wild about dates, too."

Alfred offered her some and in spite of her still slightly queasy stomach, Linn ate a couple.

When she offered Baby a date, to Linn's delight the little ferret took it delicately from Linn's fingers, ate it and came back sniffing at her fingers for more.

"I like this pet better than your snake," Linn said, stroking Baby's lithe body. The animal promptly turned over to have her belly scratched.

Looking very serious, Alfred said, "I'm sure sorry King scared you, Mrs. Randolph. He really is as gentle as Baby and wouldn't have hurt you." His face clouded and he wrinkled up his brow. "I still can't imagine how he got out of his cage and into your room that day."

Linn didn't think it wise to tell him that whoever had written the note had apparently smuggled the snake into her room or that the note had mentioned the boa.

Suddenly Linn began to feel very sick to her stomach again. Excusing herself abruptly, she went swiftly to her room. She stretched out on the bed and tried to relax, hoping the nausea would pass. Apparently the dates had not set well on her almost empty stomach.

But all at once she felt herself grow hot all over and she made a dash for the bathroom where she lost all her light breakfast and many meals before, it seemed. Feeling weak and chilly she crept back to bed, pulling the covers up to her chin. How good the bed felt! She closed her eyes.

Every muscle in her body seemed weighted and tired. Almost immediately she was asleep.

Two hours later Clay found her there.

14

Clay's voice awakened Linn. She seemed to be in a deep, black, suffocating hole and his urgent voice was slowly drawing her to the surface. Groggily she opened her eyes. Chilled when she had laid down, she had snuggled deep into the covers, but now she felt hot, disoriented. Her stomach felt like a train had run over it — leaving it flat and sore.

Beyond Clay, just inside the door, Linn saw Kate's anxious face and Penny's white, drawn countenance. Penny's face snapped Linn from her lethargic state. About two years before, Kate had been so sick the doctor hadn't been sure she would survive. Now Penny became intensely fearful if any member of the family was even slightly ill.

"Hey, you guys, I'm okay. I just had an upset stomach and . . . ," at that moment Linn's stomach lurched crazily and she felt a wave of heat travel through her body.

Scrambling from the bed she dashed to the bathroom where her stomach tried valiantly to rid itself of any remaining remnants of food or liquid she had eaten in the last month, or so it seemed.

Kate had followed her into the bathroom and now she bathed Linn's face with a cold wet cloth before helping her back to bed.

Clay sat down on the side of the bed and pushed the pale, ash-blond hair back from Linn's face with a gentle hand.

"And as for you, dear wife," he said to Linn, "you are going to the doctor!" When she started to protest, he laid a gentle finger on her lips. "That's settled — finis!"

Linn subsided. As weak as she was, it was a relief to let her strong, capable husband take command. It felt good to be cared for and coddled.

Dr. Powell was grey haired and kind. He reminded Linn of Dr. Glover, their special friend back home. After his examination, the doctor called Clay into his office.

Clay entered, looking alarmed.

With a twinkle in his eyes, Dr. Powell said, "Be seated, young man. I think your wife should tell you the news."

Puzzled, Clay turned to Linn.

Linn's gold-flecked, expressive green

eyes were glowing. "How would you like to be a father?" she asked softly.

Wonder, like a light from heaven, spread over Clay's face as he said incredulously, "Are you sure?" His eyes swung to the doctor. "You're positive?"

Linn knew what Clay was feeling. It had been their heart's desire, almost from the day they were married, to become parents. Doctors had found no reason why they could not conceive. She and Clay had consulted several, including a couple of specialists in the field. But Linn just couldn't get pregnant, it seemed. And now that the momentous happening had come to pass, it was almost more than either could believe.

"Don't put me on the spot," the doctor chuckled, "but just let me say that in my many years of experience, I haven't often been wrong."

When Clay and Linn told their news to the family, Kate and Eric were excited and happy for them, but Penny was almost beside herself with joy. She kept saying, "Just think, we're going to have a baby!"

After Linn was back home in bed and had been able to keep a little soup down, Josie came in to see her. When Linn told her about the baby and that it was the answer to a fervent prayer and desire, she was almost as excited as Penny, although naturally more subdued. Her dark eyes shone and Linn detected a wistfulness in her soft voice.

"I'm so glad for you," Josie said. "I love babies and children. That's why I want to practice pediatrics."

"And with your gentleness, you will be one of the best," Linn declared.

A slight color rose in Josie's cheeks at the praise. Always in Joe's shadow, Linn imagined Josie had never received much acclaim.

For the next several days Linn was able to keep down only small amounts of food. Dr. Powell had told her he would prescribe something to help alleviate the morning sickness if it continued to severely plague her.

But Linn soon learned what foods she could keep down most successfully and spent as much time outdoors as possible since that seemed to help. But Linn felt like the sickness was wrongly named. It wasn't just mornings that she felt bad. It was morning, noon and night, although mornings were the worst. She also had to give up the boating trips. The motion of the restless sea and her condition didn't seem to complement each other.

Their rooms were still kept locked, except for cleaning, but there had been no more problems. Everything seemed to have settled down to a comfortable, relaxed routine.

The necklace did not show up anywhere. Penny still mentioned it wistfully now and then, but even her mind was more on the new baby and the shells that she and Linn found from time to time and added to their collection.

Linn still saw the green and silver motorboat or the sailboat in the bay occasionally, but didn't let it bother her greatly. One day while walking on the beach at low tide, the green and silver motorboat pulled into their dock The redheaded man asked to make a call from the house. He seemed a nice enough fellow so Linn agreed.

Not feeling it wise to leave a stranger alone in the house, she allowed him to call from the living room phone and stayed there while he talked to someone named Molly. His call didn't seem important — just that he was out of bait and would she pick up some more for him. She wondered if it had just been an excuse to get in the house. But he didn't seem particularly curious about the interior and, after thanking her courteously, left as soon as the call was over.

The week moved forward in an un-eventful pace. Alfred had recovered from his asthma attack and still followed Penny about whenever he had the opportunity. Penny seemed to enjoy his attentions and was still impressed with his intelligence.

Eric had attended Bonnie Leeds's party and at least one other "bash" at her apart-ment, Linn knew. Clay said his only com-ment about it was, " 'Just another one of her wild parties.' "

Josie was scarcely ever seen by any of them, even Eric. Mrs. Benholt served their meals alone. It was evident that Josie was either being kept away from them or staying away of her own volition.

Eric was puzzled. He had asked Josie to join them for a singing session but she had reluctantly told him she was too busy. He confided to Linn that she had also refused to go with him to a concert in Corpus Christi which he knew she was longing to attend. They had discussed it on their last sailing date.

"I don't know if she doesn't like me or if her family's putting pressure on her to stay away from me. I can't understand it. I'm not usually considered an undesirable by young ladies or their families."

Linn almost told Eric about the conversation between Joe and Josie that she had accidentally overheard that day outside the gazebo, but she hesitated. After all, it was not their business. Josie was an adult and had to make her own choices. Besides, Eric's attentions seemed to be divided now. She wasn't sure what effect Bonnie's illusive charm might have on him.

15

Linn had known for two weeks now that she was going to be a mother. Already looking at bassinets and cribs, she had purchased two tiny gowns, and was sewing on a dainty, baby-sized quilt. Kate had shown her how.

It was late evening and today had been a very good day with little nausea. She had worked on her quilt off and on, but had also taken a long walk beachcombing on the shore with Penny.

Clay, Eric and Kate had been at the office all day today but were due home soon for dinner. It was unusual for them to work until dusk as Clay tried to keep their days short — not later than one or two o'clock each day — so there would be time for family fun together. But work had piled up and they had all three stayed late to complete it.

Linn had showered and changed for dinner. She knew Penny and Alfred were in the conservatory cleaning a few shells, and watching the antics of Alfred's dainty little ferret, so Linn decided to go up to the tower and widow's walk before dinner. With its spectacular view, it was one of her favorite places.

Linn had never gone up to the little tower this late. It was almost dark when she stepped out onto the circular walk that surrounded the tower.

Lights, like tiny, tinted stars were already twinkling in the streets of Rockport, and she could see the lights of closer houses glowing warmly here and there along the shore. Far out at sea there were also lights. *Probably a big ship's anchored there,* she thought.

It was restful and peaceful above the regal palms and windswept live-oak trees. Moving slowly along, following the circular railing, she drank in the balmy, salt-flavored night air and the view. Linn felt like she was on top of the world.

It was very quiet and it was probably the lack of noise that saved her. Suddenly, she heard a faint sound behind her and turned her head slightly to see what was there. She had just a quick, terrifying glimpse of a black figure gliding toward her with arms outstretched.

A second later something hit her in the back, knocking the breath out of her and almost sending her headlong over the railing of the tower porch. But that second's glimpse gave Linn time to grab the top of the banister and brace herself or she would have gone over, crashing to her death on the flagstones below.

Panic tore at her brain. This terrible black figure was trying to kill her!

Gasping and panting in a desperate struggle to regain her breath, and reeling from the first attack, Linn had little time to prepare before another hard blow struck her in the back. This time she almost lost her hold on the banister. She swayed, teetering out over empty space. Using her legs, feet and hands Linn fought desperately to regain her balance. Then hands were clutching at her, trying to push her gasping body over the railing.

Linn wanted to scream as terror beat in her breast, but she couldn't get enough air in her tortured lungs. She was laboring for breath and her back was throbbing with pain from the cruel blows, but her sense of self-preservation was strong. Half-turning, she grasped her assailant's clothes in a death grip with one hand while clinging desperately to the rail with the other. The attacker pulled violently away, trying to break her grip, drawing Linn away from the banister.

At that moment, Clay's voice came clearly from the foot of the steep stairs leading up to the tower. The dark figure instantly gave a hard, violent yank, broke free and darted away. Linn, still gasping painfully, slid down to the floor.

In a half-daze, she heard Clay's voice again. "Linn, are you up there?"

Taking in a great gulp of air, Linn called in a faint voice, "Clay — up — here. Clay — please —" She couldn't get any more out.

The tower light came on and Clay bounded up the stairs. At the top of the stairs, he saw Linn collapsed near the banisters, and sprang quickly to her side.

"Linn, what's wrong? What are you doing up here in the dark, on the floor?"

Suddenly the fear and horror of the past few minutes seemed to crash down upon Linn. She fell into Clay's arms, crying hysterically and shaking uncontrollably. Clay held her, soothing her with words of endearment and stroking her hair until she finally began to calm down.

"Honey, what happened?" Clay asked anxiously. "What's wrong?"

Linn raised an ashen, tear-stained face.

"Someone tried to push me off — off — the — porch." Shudders ran through her body and she began to cry again.

Clay's face registered shock, bewilderment and mounting horror. "Linn, tell me — tell me! Who tried to push you off the porch?"

"I — I don't know." Linn was starting to get a grip on herself. "I was just standing there at the railing when I heard a sound. I looked back over my shoulder and got just a quick glimpse of a dark figure before it struck me in the back. Then. . . ."

"Who was it? Did you recognize who struck you?" Clay interrupted.

"No, it was just a black shape. He must have had on a black mask, too, because I couldn't see a face, even when I grabbed hold of his clothes. He tried to push me over the rail. I almost went over, Clay." Her voice began to tremble again. "I literally hung out over the edge. I was — never — so — scared — in — my — life." Her voice had sunk to a terrified whisper. She buried her head against Clay's shoulder, her body trembling from head to toe.

Clay held her tightly. Suddenly he released her and looked into her face. "Where did he go, Linn? Did you see where he went? How could he get down those stairs without me seeing him? That's the only way down."

"Maybe he's still in the tower," Linn quavered.

Clay quickly searched the little tower room, but there was no one there.

Linn had stood shakily to her feet and when Clay came back after a moment, her face showed utter bewilderment. "But how could he have gotten past you on the stairs? He was still here when you called the first time. He pulled loose from me and ran. I still couldn't get my breath very well so I just slid down on the floor and I didn't see where he went."

"You're sure it was a man?"

Linn considered. "I really don't know. I just presumed so. I really didn't get a very good look. It all happened so fast. Whoever it was, was strong because those two blows on my back had a lot of power behind them. Clay, if you hadn't called when you did —" Her voice broke as the horror of the past few minutes washed over her afresh. She began to shake as if she were having a hard chill.

Clay wrapped his arms tightly about her and held her until the trembling began to subside. "Let's get you downstairs," Clay said gently, "and then we'll call the police."

155

Linn's face was very grave and her voice almost a whisper as she looked into Clay's face. "Do you think this has anything to do with that threatening note? Remember? It said Moonshell didn't want me — or us — here and that there would be no more warnings."

"I remember!" Clay said grimly.

The police were called and dutifully came to check out everything and to talk to everyone who was at Moonshell. No one had seen anyone or anything suspicious. The tower room was thoroughly checked as was the porch around it.

There was no clue as to who the assailant was or where he had vanished to so quickly. One police officer suggested that the attacker could have hidden in the tower, or behind it, and when Clay's full attention was focused on his wife, he could have slipped down the stairs unnoticed. Clay and Linn conceded that this could have happened.

To Joe's obvious ire, the Benholt family was questioned by the police officers as to their whereabouts at the time of the attack.

Penny could vouch for Alfred's whereabouts since he was with her in the conservatory. Joe claimed to be out in the tool shed putting away the lawnmower. Josie said she was folding laundry in the laundry room and Mrs. Benholt declared she was in the kitchen finishing dinner. Each had been alone so could not support the others' stories.

Clay took Linn to see the doctor but aside from her fright, she had suffered only a badly bruised back.

When they returned home, the family assembled in the living room for a family conference. Clay told them all that he was in favor of sending Linn, Kate and Penny back home while he and Eric moved into Corpus Christi until the shopping center was finished.

It was Linn who begged Clay not to send them home. She disliked being the cause of ruining everyone's summer vacation.

"Couldn't we just be very careful and not go into out-of-the-way places alone as I unwisely did? We can keep our doors locked when we are alone in our rooms or away. The police think it was just a prowler." She paused. "Besides, I hate to run from anything!"

Clay reluctantly said he would think about it, and pray about it, too. Linn had to be content with that.

16

In the week after the strange black figure had tried to push Linn from the tower porch, she found the terror dissipating. It had taken much prayerful trusting in God and His promises, and although she had far from forgotten, the fear was now replaced with peace.

The police had found nothing to substantiate it, but they still thought a prowler had stolen into the house and had hidden in the tower room planning to burglarize the house when everyone was asleep. They suggested that the prowler had been panicked into attacking when he thought he was about to be discovered.

Linn wanted only to put it behind her and felt that everything had now settled back to normal. She was once more basking in the joy of her motherhood.

It had been three weeks since Linn had found out about the baby. In that time she had seen almost nothing of Josie. If Linn came near her, she only smiled and hurried away. So it was with a good deal of surprise that Linn answered a knock on her door one Saturday morning and saw Josie standing there. When Linn invited her in, she looked both ways down the hall and then quickly slipped inside. Josie appeared nervous and distraught.

Linn motioned Josie to a cushioned chair and plopped herself back in bed with big pillows at her back. "How have you been, Josie?" she began, knowing this was not a social call but trying to put the agitated girl at ease.

Josie tried to speak but before she got out one word her face crumpled. She put her head in her hands and began to sob in shuddering, tearing grief.

Linn was instantly at her side. Kneeling beside her, Linn put her arms about Josie and held her trembling body, murmuring soothingly to her. Frightening thoughts spun around in her mind. Had something terrible happened? Or was Josie under so much pressure she was having a nervous breakdown? It must be a personal matter or she would surely have just blurted it right out.

Finally Josie, with great effort it seemed,

stopped crying. But she was still trembling. When she drew away, looking embarrassed and contrite, Linn saw that there were dark circles under her eyes.

"I-I'm sorry," Josie said, dabbing at her eyes with the tissues Linn had pressed into her cold hand. "I never let go like this. I don't know what got into me." She looked into Linn's sympathetic face for a minute and then she burst out angrily, "Yes I do! You are always s-so sweet and s-so caring. I'm just not used to anyone like that."

She was about to cry again but bit her lip and waited a moment until she had herself back under control before she spoke.

"My mother and brothers love me . . . I think." Tears threatened again but she forced them back. "But we are not an affectionate family." She tried to smile but it came out all crooked. "But I'm taking up your time so I'll cut out the pity-party. I came to ask you for some advice. I just don't know what to do."

"What is the problem?" Linn asked gently.

Josie dropped her eyes and studied her hands which were unconsciously shredding the tissues they held. "I feel so disloyal to my family when I go to an outsider, b-but I just don't know what to do!" When she looked at Linn, her soft dark eyes were pools of intense anguish.

"What you tell me will be kept in the strictest confidence," Linn promised her.

Josie took a deep breath, "I knew it would be. And I have to tell someone!"

"Sometimes it helps to just talk things out," Linn encouraged.

"I hardly know where to start," Josie said, "but do you recall what I told you about Joe insisting that I become a surgeon?"

"Yes, and that your desire is to be a pediatrician."

"That's right. And also Joe isn't pleased that I dated Eric and that I like you all. He even resents my joining your singing sessions."

"Do you know why?"

"He gives me reasons but I don't think they are the real reasons. Joe has always been bigger and stronger than me. For some strange reason, it seems important to him to be able to do everything better than I can."

"And that's why Joe resents your singing with us?"

"I believe so. He can't carry a tune. That's the only thing I can do that he can't. At home, it's okay if I sing. Nobody hears me or compliments me," she said matter of factly.

"You do have a beautiful voice," Linn said warmly.

Josie glowed under the compliment. "When we were children, a teacher once gave me the singing lead in a musical play. Joe told Mother it wasn't fair that I got to practice every day after school and he had to work. Of course Mother took me out of the play. I don't think she liked girls very much, and Joe was always her favorite. She's never mistreated me, just ignored me."

"Perhaps she has been so busy trying to make a living, she hasn't realized she neglected you," Linn suggested gently.

"Perhaps. Although she always had time for Joe and Alfred. But enough of this! I still haven't told you my quandary and Mother will soon miss me and come searching.

"The day you got sick, a couple of weeks ago, Joe gave me an ultimatum. If I did not stop seeing Eric and persisted in refusing to specialize in surgery, he would confiscate all the money in our joint bank account and I would have no money to start school with this fall."

Josie's lips began to tremble and she

caught her lower lip between even white teeth to still their quivering before she went on. "Practicing medicine has been my lifelong dream. So, since it seemed I had no choice, I have tried to comply with Joe's demands."

Linn laid a slim, warm hand on Josie's arm in sympathy.

Josie's voice shook as she continued, "But, I feel like I am suffocating! I never had any real friends before you came to Moonshell. Joe saw to that. But now I have had a taste of what it means to have good clean fun and fellowship with some fine people and I am no longer contented with my life.

"Linn," her words were a cry of anguish, "am I wrong? I love my family but they just aren't enough. I want a life of my own!"

Linn prayed silently for guidance before she answered. "Josie, I feel that you should do what you want to do. No one has the right to dictate how we live our lives but God. Have you prayed about all of this, Josie?"

Josie's eyes were riveted to Linn's face. "I don't really know how to pray. My church doesn't teach praying spontaneously like yours does. And none of my memorized prayers cover this situation.

"Joe and Mother forbade me to go to your church but after I went there just that once I felt so peaceful and good. Your pastor said God wants to be real and personal but He isn't to me. I just hurt down here to have what you have." She laid a small, shapely hand over her heart.

Impulsively Linn said, "Tomorrow is Sunday. Why don't you go to church with us again. Your spiritual life is no one's concern but your own."

Josie looked away from Linn for a moment as if she were in deep thought. When she swung her eyes back, Linn saw an eager light burning there. Josie opened her lips to speak — and there was a knock on the door.

Instantly Josie sprang to her feet. "It must be Mother," she whispered. "I've stayed too long. I don't want her to know I have been here."

Linn motioned toward the French doors. "Go out that way, and I'll cover for you," she whispered with a conspiratorial grin.

Josie smiled. "Thanks so much for everything! And I'm going with you Sunday night!" she whispered as she slipped away.

There was another tap at the door and an urgent voice called, "Mrs. Randolph, I need Josie. Is she in your room?"

Linn went leisurely to the door. Before Mrs. Benholt could say another word, she said, "No, Josie isn't here, but when you find her, would you send her to my room? There is some sand on the carpet that I accidentally spilled out of my shoe." It was a legitimate excuse and Linn was glad now that she had been careless.

Mrs. Benholt's eyes swept over the interior of Linn's room before she promised to return promptly herself and vacuum up the sand.

17

Eric's attendance at church had been minimal since the cookout when Pastor Haskins had urged him to accept Christ. As a matter of fact, Linn realized that she hadn't seen much of him at all lately. But when Linn informed him that Josie was going to church with them Sunday evening, Eric quickly decided to go, too.

The pastor didn't know that Josie was coming so Linn marveled at the topic of his sermon Sunday night, "God Is Your Answer." He explained that there was no problem, large or small, that God was not concerned about. But in order for God to intervene in one's life, that person must first unreservedly give his or her life to God and then place the problem totally into His capable hands.

Linn was disappointed that Josie did not go forward when the pastor gave the invitation. She did notice that Eric was very attentive to the sermon, but he didn't respond by going forward, either.

After the service was dismissed and everyone was moving slowly up the aisle toward the doorway where the minister was shaking hands with the congregation, Josie suddenly whispered to Linn, "Do you suppose the pastor would have time to answer some questions for me?"

Linn's heart did a flip-flop but she managed to answer calmly, "I'll ask him if you want me to."

"Would you?" Josie said gratefully.

Pastor Haskins not only was delighted to answer Josie's questions, but he insisted on all of them coming next door to the parsonage where they could be more comfortable.

Kate had some things to do before she retired, though, so she and Penny drove home in Clay's car. Eric promised to bring Josie, Linn and Clay home later.

Ellen Haskins put coffee on to perk and stuck some homemade cinnamon rolls in the oven to heat before she hustled her two little girls from the room. Linn and Josie went with her to the girls' bedroom and helped dress the children for bed. Josie even sang them a little song before their mother tucked the lively youngsters into bed.

The questions Josie asked, as the adults sat in the comfortable living room a few minutes later, were simple and direct. "How do I give my life to Christ? Could it be that simple? What does God expect from me? Will God really help me to choose the right path for my life? How can I *know?*"

After about an hour of discussion, Josie did not wait to be asked if she wished to pray. With an eager light in her dark eyes, she stated that she was ready to commit her life to God. With the pastor helping her to pray, she confessed her sin and need of a Savior, and invited Christ into her life. When she lifted her head from prayer, her face was radiant.

"Remember, Josie," cautioned Pastor Haskins as they were getting ready to leave, "regardless of how you feel tomorrow or at a later date, you are a child of God and God is with you.

"Sometimes, when things aren't going well for us, we're inclined to believe God has forsaken us or we were never really children of God. But we don't walk by feelings. We walk by faith in God's Word which says if we ask Him to forgive us, He does just that."

Eric didn't participate during the discussion, listening intently to all that was said. Linn had so hoped he would follow Josie's example and give his life to the Lord. But even though he bowed his head in reverence when the others prayed, Eric made no move toward God himself.

Before they retired for the night, Linn and Clay fervently thanked God for Josie's salvation and prayed that God would give her the necessary strength to stand for God in her home. They knew it would not be easy for her.

But they were not prepared for the drastic measures the Benholts would take.

Clay had just left for work the next morning and Linn had crawled back into bed since she felt a bit queasy when Josie tapped on Linn's door.

As soon as Linn opened the door and saw Josie's face, she knew something serious was wrong. Josie's face was ashen and she seemed almost to be in a state of shock. Linn drew her into the room and gently pushed her into a chair, drawing up a chair for herself close by.

"What's wrong, Josie?" she asked, when Josie just sat there as if in a daze.

"They're turning me out," Josie said woodenly.

"Turning you out? Who's turning you out?"

Tears began to run down Josie's face but she didn't seem aware of them. "Joe said that since I had chosen to separate myself from the Benholt family, I was to pack my things and get out! And M-Mother just turned her back on me and walked out when I looked to her for help."

Josie began to tremble. "Linn, what am I going to do? I don't know how to make it on my own. Where am I going to g-go?"

Linn took Josie's cold hands in her own warm ones. "Josie, you still have a job. Remember, my husband pays your salary. And this is a big house with many empty rooms. We'll just move your things into one of them."

Wonder and renewed hope dawned in Josie's eyes. "I guess I had forgotten that Mr. Randolph is my boss. Joe or Mother has always gotten my money and just given me a little for my personal expenses. I guess I always considered myself employed by them."

She looked up anxiously into Linn's face. "I don't want to be a burden to you or your husband. I shouldn't have come running to you now, but I was simply petrified with fear when Joe said they had disowned me and I had to leave. That's what he said. Disowned!"

"You were right to come to me," Linn said emphatically. "And you have every right to collect and handle your own money. Tomorrow is payday, if I remember correctly. I'll see to it that your wages are paid to you personally.

"With room and board furnished, you should be able to bank most of your salary for college. And I know that grants and loans are available for responsible students."

Josie suddenly leaned forward and hugged Linn. "You make my being tossed out into the big, cold world almost like a great adventure," she said shakily. "And maybe it is just what I need to make me rely on myself and God. But it's still the most frightening experience of my life."

"I don't doubt it," Linn said.

"How can I ever repay you for helping me —" Josie began, but Linn interrupted her.

"I really haven't done anything," Linn said. "You are strong, healthy and intelligent. You can make your own way. Clay and I are your friends and will be glad to help in any way we can. And don't forget that you have God on your side. The whole world is your oyster!

"Now, why don't you go pack your things while I prepare a room for you."

Linn chose a room beyond Kate's and Penny's rooms which had a private bath and was nicely furnished. When Josie returned with an armload of clothes on hangers, Linn told her to help herself to sheets, blankets and towels from the large linen closet on that floor. She helped Josie stow her rather meager wardrobe and personal belongings in her new quarters. In less than an hour the job was completed.

"I'll go talk to your mother," Linn said, "and tell her that I would like you to be in charge of cleaning our rooms up here and helping to serve our meals as you used to do. Is that agreeable with you?"

"Of course. And, Linn, thank you!"

Linn gave her a quick hug and went to get dressed.

Linn tried to be diplomatic when she approached the housekeeper. "Mrs. Benholt, I understand there has been a little problem in your family. But we still want to retain Josie in our employ, so I have invited her to move into our part of the house. Josie will be cleaning our rooms on the second floor and I have asked her to help with the meal serving, also.

"She will look to me for her duties but I

will consult with you on cleaning and other things which need done. I hope that is okay with you?"

Mrs. Benholt stood stiff and unsmiling during Linn's discourse. Now she said grudgingly, "You're the boss, Mrs. Randolph. But I wish you hadn't interfered in our family problems. Josie's place is with her family."

Linn raised an inquiring eyebrow. "I understood you had asked her to leave?"

"She knows she can stay if she straightens up and does what she is told to do," Mrs. Benholt replied sullenly.

"Your daughter is a twenty-three-year-old adult, Mrs. Benholt. Perhaps it is time she tried her wings."

Mrs. Benholt grunted something indiscernible and excused herself to her duties.

Linn wondered if Clay would be unhappy with her for not waiting to consult with him, but he agreed that she had done the only thing she could have done under the circumstances. She was relieved. But the bad news of the day wasn't over. As they gathered in the dining room before dinner that night, Linn realized that Eric was absent again.

When Clay joined her at the dining table, she could see that he seemed preoccupied. Clay hadn't mentioned why Eric hadn't come home, so she asked, "Where's Eric?"

Clay looked up from his soup. "He didn't say where he was going when he left the office tonight. Just said he had to meet someone." And changed the subject.

All through dinner Clay wasn't quite himself. His remoteness disturbed Linn. Usually Clay confided in her if something was troubling him, but he didn't like to be quizzed until he got ready to tell her what was on his mind. Knowing her husband well, Linn tactfully avoided pressuring him and directed the conversation into other channels.

Later in the week, while dressing for a dinner party at the Molinas's, Clay was again withdrawn, almost taciturn.

"Doesn't the mother of your soon-to-be-son get a kiss tonight?" Linn teased.

Clay didn't smile. In fact, he didn't seem to hear her.

Linn stood just inside their door for a moment and watched him. At first she felt a surge of indignation at the lack of attention, then her better sense took over. She knew he was deeply distressed or disturbed about something. Not wanting to force his confidence, Linn quietly finished dressing, but cast several worried looks at Clay.

When they were all ready to leave for the Molinas's dinner party, Linn realized that Eric had not yet come home. Now she was almost certain that whatever had Clay so glum was related to Eric.

When Josie came down the hall, looking pretty as a doll in a soft pink and white dress, Linn could see her eyes quickly scan the group. Realizing that Eric wasn't there, she sought out Clay. "Isn't Eric coming?" she asked.

Clay took his time about answering, but finally said slowly, "I don't know. He didn't come home with me. Said he had to meet someone downtown. Perhaps he plans to meet us over at the Molinas's house later."

Josie seemed content with that and went on out to the car. But Linn wasn't. Putting her hand on Clay's arm, Linn stopped him from going out the door. "Clay, what's going on? You've been preoccupied since you came home and now Eric doesn't show up for a date with Josie. And I know he didn't call. That's not like him and it's not like you either."

Clay drew in a long, troubled breath. "I don't like to jump to conclusions," he said, "so I don't know what to say. I don't want to be wrong."

"Wrong about what?" Linn asked.

"Eric." Clay looked away from Linn's anxious green eyes. "Eric got a phone call about ten o'clock this morning. He didn't say who it was but I think it was from someone he met at one of Bonnie's parties. When he hung up, he didn't say anything about it, so I just forgot it. But when we were ready to leave for home, Eric told me abruptly that he was meeting someone and wouldn't be going home with me. Then he hurried out the door before I could say anything.

"Linn, I hope I'm wrong, but I really don't think Eric will show up this evening. He acted very secretive about who called and his plans. And secrecy is so foreign to Eric. He's always told me about his business and his girls — even those he knows I disapprove of.

"Don't mention this to Josie. Maybe Eric will come to dinner and you can lecture me later about my wild imagination." Clay tried to smile, but it came out as more of a grimace and Linn knew how worried Clay really was.

In fact, Eric didn't come home at all that night. And the next day he only stopped by long enough to pick up a few of his clothes. When Clay asked him bluntly what the problem was, Eric said he'd rather not discuss it and stalked out of the house.

18

The new household arrangements worked out better than Linn had expected. Mrs. Benholt said as little to Josie as possible when she helped serve the meals, but since she usually said little to her anyway, it wasn't too uncomfortable for Josie.

Joe always managed to be as far away from Linn or any of her family as possible, but he continued to do his work conscientiously. Josie told Linn, however, that he would not speak to her or even look at her. Linn saw the hurt in her eyes. She wondered how much of it was related to Eric. She knew he had been avoiding all of them as much as possible but didn't feel free to broach the subject to Josie. Instead, she urged Josie to petition God about her problems, assuring her that He could work miracles.

"Without God's help, I could never have borne the rejection by my family," Josie said. "It still hurts but knowing that God cares, and that I have friends who care, makes it bearable. But I'm praying for a reconciliation with everyone I care about."

Alfred didn't appear to be affected by the estrangement within his family. He still continued to spend as much time with Penny as he could. Also, he never avoided any of her family members as his brother and mother obviously did. He was cheerful and helpful and invited himself on Linn's and Penny's shell-collecting jaunts whenever he could wrangle an invitation.

Linn was still queasy sometimes in the mornings but not nearly as bad as she had been at first. And, unless she became upset, she was almost never sick in the afternoons. She was beginning to feel like her old healthy self again.

She was thankful the medication for morning sickness had been unnecessary. Her doctor disliked giving expectant mothers any kind of medication unless it was badly needed in case it might have an adverse effect on the unborn baby. Linn and Clay were in total agreement.

Three days after Josie had moved into the main part of the house, Linn felt quite well when she woke up and had gone down to see Clay off to work. However, the odor of the beautifully browned sausage Mrs. Benholt had prepared to go with the pancakes and maple syrup for breakfast set Linn's stomach to rolling. She doggedly refused to leave the table, but sipped a little ginger ale, hoping the nausea would pass.

After Clay and Eric had left for work, Linn decided to go back to bed. It was only seven o'clock and both Kate and Penny were apparently sleeping in.

The first thing Linn spied when she reached her room was a cute little sea chest tied with a bright red ribbon. She knew what it would contain before she untied the colorful ribbon. Her throat constricted with pleasure as she slipped off the gay ribbon and opened the lid. Rows of rich, dark golden-brown dates were packed in the chest.

Dear Clay, she thought. Knowing her love for dates, he had bought her the gooey fruit many times since they had been married. Packaged in boxes, packages and even bags, he had always tied whatever container they came in with a bright red ribbon. *What could be more fitting*, she thought, *for the first dates Clay has given me at Moonshell than a sea chest full of the golden goodies.*

I wish I dared eat one, but I had better wait

until after lunch when my stomach is usually in pretty good shape.

So Linn settled down in bed to read. An hour later Penny tapped on her door. When Linn called, Penny stuck her head in the door. "Linn, do you want to go on a picnic? Mother said she feels like running down to Mustang Island and playing around in the surf."

"Sure, why not," Linn quickly agreed. "Clay and Eric won't be in until evening today."

"Is it okay if Alfred comes?"

"Certainly, if Aunt Kate doesn't care."

"She doesn't, I've already asked. I'll go see if he wants to go."

Penny was about to go bouncing off when Linn suddenly remembered her gift of dates. "Wait, Penny. Take a couple of dates for Alfred's little ferret."

Penny wrinkled up her nose. "How you and Baby can like those things is more than I know." But she took the dates and darted away after obtaining Linn's promise to be ready in thirty minutes.

Ten minutes later, Linn joined Kate at the dining table. Her stomach felt like she might be able to eat some toast and orange juice. Over breakfast they were talking companionably about the plans for the day when Penny came running from the direction of the kitchen. Her emerald eyes were wide with fright.

"Come quick!" she called frantically. "There's something wrong with Baby!" And she darted away out the side entrance where they could hear her urgently calling Joe.

Linn and Kate dashed through the kitchen and into the Benholt apartment. Alfred was kneeling on the floor, his face as pasty white as Penny's, tensely watching Josie working over the limp form of Alfred's pet.

Linn stared in mounting horror. Baby was very still and did not seem to even be breathing!

Joe charged into the room and took over the rescue efforts, even to giving mouth to mouth resuscitation, but to no avail. He finally stood up with the small furry form in his browned hands. "She's dead, Alfred. I'm sorry, there just wasn't anything we could do."

Alfred reached numbly for his pet and hugged her small limp form to his chest. His eyes looked glazed with unbelief. "But she can't be dead. Just a few minutes ago, she was running all around and when Penny fed her the dates, she started eating like she wasn't sick at all!"

"She was eating a date when she started getting sick?" Joe asked.

"Yeah, and before she even got through the second one, she started twisting and clawing at her throat like she couldn't breathe good. That's when I yelled for Josie and she came running."

Joe turned to Josie. "Do you think she has a date seed caught in her throat?"

Josie shook her head. "That's what I thought, but Alfred said there was no seed in the dates. He had squeezed them both to see before Penny fed them to the ferret. And I looked down her throat. There wasn't any obstruction."

"But the ferret got sick while eating a date?" He seemed to be talking more to himself than anyone else, but Alfred answered.

"Before she even got the second one eaten. They never made her sick before!"

"Alfred, where did you get the dates?" Mrs. Benholt suddenly interjected.

"Mrs. Randolph sent them with Penny for Baby."

All eyes turned to Linn but Linn could only see Alfred's eyes, anguished and beginning to fill with tears that he self-consciously dashed away.

"There couldn't be anything wrong with the dates!" Linn exclaimed. "Clay bought them for me."

"They're the same ones you've been eating?" Joe asked slowly.

"Yes! Well — no. Clay just left them for me this morning — in my room. I was somewhat nauseous so I hadn't eaten one yet."

"Why don't you go get them so we can check them," Joe said.

"What are you thinking?" Linn exclaimed. "There couldn't be anything wrong with them. Clay gave them to me!"

"They could be contaminated with insecticide or anything," Joe said.

Penny volunteered to go for the dates and was quickly back with the pretty little sea chest. When opened, Joe conceded that they looked all right but suggested that none be eaten until they were checked.

"Let's consult Clay before we do anything," Linn said, remembering how provoked Clay had been with the way she handled the last incident.

Linn dialed the number and when Clay's secretary answered, she asked for Clay. In a moment Linn heard his voice on the line.

"Linn, is anything wrong?"

"Yes, Clay, and we don't know what to

make of it. Alfred's little ferret, Baby, ate a couple of those dates you left for me and —"

"What dates?"

"The ones you left for me this morning on my bedside table. You know, in the little sea chest, tied with a red ribbon like you always —"

Clay's voice cut in, "I didn't leave you any dates — anywhere!"

Shock and fear spread through Linn's veins like ice water. She felt light-headed and nausea threatened again. She could hear Clay's voice as if it were far off.

"Linn — Linn, are you still there?"

"Yes — yes, I'm still here."

"Tell me what is going on there. You said Baby ate two dates from a sea chest you thought I left you?"

"Yes, and Baby is dead! She died while eating the second date!"

"Did you eat any of the dates, Linn?" Clay's voice sounded strained and unnatural.

"No, I would have but I felt queasy this morning."

"Thank God! No one else ate any, did they?"

"No."

"Don't let anyone even touch those

dates! Have Kate bring them in to me immediately and bring Alfred's little ferret, too. On second thought, I think you and Penny had better come also. I don't want you alone in that house!"

Linn replaced the telephone with a shaking hand and turned to face the circle of anxious faces.

Kate spoke before Linn could say a word, "Clay didn't give you those dates." It was a declaration.

Linn nodded. "He knew nothing about them. He wants us to go into Corpus Christi and bring the dates — and also the ferret. He wants to have them checked." She turned to Alfred. "Do you mind if we take Baby?"

"That's a good idea," Joe agreed. "At least this is one time we Benholts won't be blamed! Anyone knows we wouldn't have killed our own ferret."

"Joe!" Josie said, shocked.

Joe answered resentfully, "Well, it's the truth. Every bad thing that happens, we get the credit for it!" His eyes took on a spiteful look. "Not you, of course, just the rest of the clan!"

"You're impossible!" Josie said, on the verge of tears.

Linn felt like telling him off, but she

185

clamped her lips together determinedly. This was no time to be fighting.

"Can I go with you?" Alfred broke in, looking at Linn with pleading eyes.

"Of course," Linn said, "and Clay wanted us to come immediately."

"I would like to go, too, if I may," Joe said, surprising Linn. "I want to know what's wrong with those dates."

19

As they drove over the now familiar highway to Corpus Christi with Kate at the wheel, Alfred still held his little ferret in his arms, wrapped in part of an old blanket. Even Penny could not induce him to say more than a brief answer to a direct question.

Linn's heart ached for the sensitive boy. She realized she had grown very fond of him. Mrs. Benholt's whispered, "He raised that ferret from a baby and it is very dear to him," didn't help Linn's feelings. She felt somehow responsible for Alfred's grief. Even though they didn't know for sure yet that the dates had been responsible for Baby's death, it certainly looked that way.

Linn tried not to think of how the dates had gotten into her room. That was something she didn't want to deal with yet. The room had been securely locked — and with the new locks for which even the Benholts did not have a key!

By late that afternoon they knew the dates had been poisoned. The dates contained a large amount of tetradoxin, a deadly poison extracted from the puffer fish. Mr. Fisher, a chemist who was recommended to Clay, had asked Alfred and Penny how the little ferret had acted. He had taken tests of a strange substance he found in the dates and fed the information into a computer. The results showed that there was enough poison in one date to kill an adult human. Mr. Fisher explained that tetradoxin affected the respiratory center in the brain and resulted in paralysis of the respiratory muscles. Baby had suffocated!

It was a solemn party that returned to Moonshell that evening. As they got out of the car, Linn laid her hand on Alfred's arm. "Alfred, I am so sorry about your ferret. I. . . ."

A spasm of pain touched his face and then Alfred answered gravely, "I'm awful sorry about Baby, too. But coming home I've been thinking. If Baby hadn't eaten a date before you did, you might be dead now instead of Baby. And a person is far more important than an animal." He smiled his shy grin, and Linn suddenly had a lump as big as a baseball in her throat.

The police had accompanied them

home. Everyone told their stories, and the police searched Clay and Linn's bedroom. But again they could find no clues. There were not even any strange fingerprints in their bedroom.

Clay asked the Benholts to stay for a few minutes after the police left with the sea chest of dates. Joe looked angry and muttered something under his breath but he stayed.

"I'm not accusing anyone of anything," Clay said, with a significant glance at Joe, "but I thought if we all just talked, we might come up with something the police missed. First of all, Joe, you told the police that you saw no one around the house. Not even the maids were here today?"

"That's right," Joe said sullenly. "I saw no one. And it's the maids' day off. But no one can get in your rooms anyway. We don't have a key and neither do the day maids."

Clay turned to Linn, "And you're sure our rooms were locked, even the French doors?"

"Positive! I remember thinking what a nuisance it was to unlock a room every time I wanted to enter it."

Clay looked thoughtful, "So the question is, how did someone get into our locked rooms?

"Is there a way to get into our bedroom without using the doors or windows?" Clay asked the group as a whole. When no one answered, he looked at Joe. "Joe, do you know of a secret door, or something of that sort, into our rooms?"

Joe's eyes mirrored hostility, "This is an old house. There could be one but I don't know if there is."

Alfred was sitting near Joe and Linn saw a strange expression register in his eyes as Joe answered. Was it shock?

"Alfred, what about you?" Clay asked quickly.

Alfred's face turned red. He glanced at Joe, then at Clay and then down at his feet.

"I don't fool around in the main house much," he muttered.

"But maybe you've heard stories about a secret door," Clay urged, sure that Alfred knew more than he was telling.

"No, I don't remember anyone mentioning one."

"I have been the housekeeper at Moonshell for many years, Mr. Randolph," Mrs. Benholt said a little tartly, "and I never heard of a secret door anywhere in it!"

"Nor I," Josie added. "But it is frightening to think that some strange person can get into any of our rooms without being seen."

"Of course, a professional burglar would have no problem," Joe said dryly.

"This person is not a burglar," Clay said. "Whoever it is has attempted to murder my wife twice. I don't plan to give him another chance. My wife, Kate and Penny will be going home as soon as they can get packed. Eric and I will move into Corpus Christi for the rest of the summer."

He said good night to the Benholts, who seemed shocked that everyone would be leaving. Eric, who had come in as the police were leaving, helped Clay carefully search Kate's and Penny's quarters before they went to bed and advised them to lock their doors.

Then they carefully examined the walls of the Randolph suite before Clay and Linn retired for the night. They found nothing that resembled a secret panel or opening.

Clay was surprised that Linn went to sleep so quickly. But he knew she possessed the ability to trust the family, herself and their problems into God's hands. He had seen her do it often and almost envied her childlike faith. He was trying to develop the same trust but still struggled at times.

He lay for a long time, troubled and fearful. He realized that twice in the past short while someone had tried to kill Linn. It was terrifying. And the horrible part of it all was that unless they could find out who, there was no way to protect his wife. She was not even safe behind locked doors because either someone had the key or there was another way into this room!

Unable to rest, Clay softly climbed out of bed. Quietly, he walked out through the French doors onto the porch and went to lean on the railing. It was a glorious night. The moon's silver crescent seemed nestled in the deep velvet blue of the night. The stars glittered like jewels. A gentle, balmy breeze brought the scent of jasmine to his nostrils. The sound of the waves rolling up onto the sands and the soft, nighttime twitterings of birds roosting in a huge, windswept live-oak tree nearby, cast their peaceful balm over the night.

Clay suddenly felt a yearning sadness. Moonshell was so beautiful! It would be a shame to have to cut short their stay here. This had been a marvelous vacation for all of them. Linn, Kate and Penny were getting lovely tans and everyone seemed to be enjoying the coast so much. But too much was happening, and even though he hadn't told Linn, he was still deeply troubled about Eric. Just the evening before he had seen a jet-setter redhead of Bonnie's caliber pick Eric up at noon in a red convertible. He hadn't returned all day.

He knew Linn was distressed, both at his silence and Eric's erratic behavior. He could see the pain and questions in Josie's eyes on the infrequent occasions she and Eric were in the same room.

Nothing was making sense anymore. But the quiet of the night was soothing the worried frown from his face. It was growing quite late and Clay decided to go back to bed. Maybe he could sleep now. But he lingered for a few more minutes soaking in the deep peace of the night.

Looking up into the star-sprinkled sky, he talked to God for awhile. Suddenly his heart was full of praise. Praise to God for giving him thoughtful, sweet, full-of-fun Linn for a wife. Praise that through her, he, Clay Randolph, the intellectual, sophisticated, unbelieving agnostic had found God — and found Him unbelievably precious and satisfying. The praise arrested his thoughts. He could trust God to work in Eric's heart, too.

"And thank you for protecting Linn," Clay prayed softly. "None of this makes sense to us, but you know all about it. Keep your hand of protection upon this whole household, but especially Linn. For some crazy reason she seems to be the target of this mischief."

Clay could feel the tension ease out of him. He looked at his watch. It was one o'clock in the morning. He turned and went inside knowing that now he could sleep.

20

The next morning Linn awoke with a dull headache, her muscles sore and aching. She felt moody and grumpy. *I could lay it on my "condition,"* she thought, *but I really know what has put me in the doldrums — Eric and Josie and the possibility that we will have to leave Moonshell.*

Eric's erratic behavior worried her. He had been home only infrequently, and he hadn't come to church or called the pastor.

Linn knew that Clay and Eric had daily contact on the job but Clay had lamented to Linn this morning before he left that his friend was uncommunicative and distant toward him.

"He suddenly seems transported into another world," Clay said, deeply troubled, "and he won't let me in. In all the years I have known Eric, he has never been like this. It's as if that new girlfriend has be- witched him," he said savagely.

"Girlfriend?" Linn exclaimed.

Clay nodded and told her about the red-head — and his midnight ponderings.

"I can't understand it," Linn said. "He seemed so near to coming to God and seemed so crazy about Josie. I know she's broken-hearted!"

"I could just wring Eric's neck," Clay said vehemently. "I shudder to think what this may do to Josie."

"I know," Linn said, "but let's not give up on either of them. God is still God and He still answers prayer."

"Thanks for reminding me," Clay said with a shadow of his old smile. "I know worry is the opposite of faith. Let's talk to our heavenly Father about this and believe for the best to come out of it." Joining hands, they prayed briefly together. Then, squaring his shoulders, Clay left for work.

After Clay left, Linn had gone back to sleep but now wished she hadn't. The extra sleep had made her feel groggy. *I must leave Eric and Josie in God's capable hands as we prayed a while ago,* she thought.

Her thoughts went to what Clay had said about Josie. Linn, too, was more than a little anxious about her. Josie seemed to be withdrawing further and further into a shell. Her eyes looked haunted and she seemed to be dying a little more each day that dragged on without Eric contacting her in any way.

Linn tried to talk to her but Josie shied away, saying she didn't feel like talking. She avoided Linn whenever possible, but Linn cornered her that morning and urged her to turn the whole thing over to God.

Josie looked at Linn with tortured eyes and replied, "I don't think God hears me anymore. Don't think I haven't prayed! I have prayed and prayed and prayed! But the heavens seem shut to me!" Josie almost broke down then but checked herself with great effort.

"Go on and cry," Linn urged gently. "Tears were given to us as sort of a pop-off valve. When the pressure or sorrow gets too great, crying can bring a release."

"I'll not be a crybaby!" Josie said fiercely. "You warned me and so did Joe, repeatedly, but I had to go and make a complete fool of myself so I've no one to blame but myself! Joe is really rubbing it in for not listening to him," she said caustically, "but I guess I have it coming."

"You haven't!" Linn said angrily. "And it is cruel for him to goad you about Eric. This could have happened to any girl! I could just shake Eric! He led you to believe he cared for you. And I could shake Joe, too!"

"Thank you, Linn," Josie said with quiet dignity. "I appreciate your concern for me but I don't want your pity. I'll survive this and I will be a much wiser girl the next time," she finished bitterly. "Now, I must get back to work."

If Josie is surviving, it's a meager living, Linn speculated, watching her hurry away. Josie seemed to be wasting away before their very eyes. She had lost weight she could ill afford to lose since she was tiny to begin with, and she went about her work like a zombie, silent and unsmiling although still a conscientious worker. Indeed, she seemed to be trying to lose herself in work. Linn had chided Josie that she was working too hard but she had only murmured something about wanting to do her share and continued to drive herself.

Sighing deeply, Linn went down to breakfast. While eating she and Penny decided to search for shells. Linn asked Mrs. Benholt's permission for Alfred to run her and Penny over to an island in the small motorboat.

She gave it willingly but cautioned them to be careful. "There's a storm out in the Gulf so the waves will be higher and the currents much stronger." They promised to be careful, packed a picnic lunch and planned to spend the entire day.

When Alfred beached the small craft on the sand, he and Penny eagerly jumped out and ran down the beach, searching for shells and other bounty the sea might have deposited on the shore.

Linn spread a towel on the sand and sank down, relaxing gratefully in the warmth of the sun. Sea gulls wheeled in the sky above. Their raucous cries above the sound of the surf lent a certain carefree feeling to the deserted beach.

It wasn't really deserted, though. Little spindle-legged birds scurried about the water's edge, searching for food. A pelican was diving for his breakfast, and a lone great blue heron rose into the air with a great beating of wings, flapping away to land in a tall, skeletal tree.

Breathing deeply of the tangy, briny air, Linn was glad she had come. Already her spirits had lifted and her headache had gone. The frightening events faded like a bad nightmare. Even their impending return to Grey Oaks couldn't affect her today. It felt good to simply enjoy the beauty before her as if she hadn't a care in the world.

Her thoughts stopped unexpectedly to explore this idea in her mind. She really didn't have a care in the world! She had cast her cares on the Lord.

"Father, all my worries about Eric and Josie, the danger that seems to be haunting Moonshell — Clay and I prayed about them this morning. Forgive me for taking them back! I relinquish them all into your hands," Linn prayed aloud softly.

With a light heart, she removed her shoes and waded out into the rolling waves. It felt good to be alive!

Late that afternoon Alfred steered the small motorboat into the Moonshell canal and cruised slowly toward the boathouse.

"Who's that up on the tower?" Penny asked, shielding her eyes with a tanned hand.

Alfred squinted upward. "It's just Josie. I remember she was wearing a blue and white dress today."

Linn glanced up at the widow's walk and saw that it was, indeed, Josie up there. She was standing at the railing. Idly, Linn wondered why Josie was up on the tower.

But she forgot Josie as the small boat docked. Linn watched as Alfred solicitously helped Penny alight from the boat like she was a delicate china doll instead of an agile, healthy teenager, and smiled. She no longer felt a dislike or distrust for Alfred. He was an intelligent, responsible, and altogether lovable boy. She was glad he and Penny were good friends.

The small segment of bad kids in our society get far too much attention, she reflected. *Courteous, obedient teens like Alfred and Penny and some of the other young people I've met at church seldom receive any publicity but they will be the pillars of the nation in the future.*

Alfred helped Linn from the boat, pulling her from her reverie, and then gathered up the picnic hamper and other paraphernalia. With Penny and Linn assisting him, they carried everything into the house in one trip.

"We can clean these later," Linn told Penny and Alfred, depositing their shells in the conservatory sink in some water. "I'm just too tired to do them now."

Penny and Alfred insisted on cleaning them, so Linn let them and went upstairs to rest a bit before dinner. She stretched out on the comfortable waterbed and relaxed with a sigh.

But something was right in the edge of her memory and wouldn't let her rest.

Suddenly she sat bolt upright on her

bed. Josie! Josie was always in the kitchen at this hour, helping with dinner! So what was she doing on the tower roof? Horror, like a ghastly octopus, wrapped its vice-like tentacles about her heart. Her mouth went dry! The tower would be an excellent place to commit suicide!

Linn leaped off the bed, not stopping for her shoes, and dashing out into the hall, she raced down the corridor. Her bare feet scarcely touched the treads of the stairs as she charged up to the tower, praying with every step.

As she ran, wild thoughts ran rampant in her mind. Josie wouldn't really take her own life, would she? But Josie's suffering, anguished eyes rose in Linn's mind and she put on another burst of speed. *Eric, how could you do this to Josie?* her mind screamed.

The widow's walk was built atop the tower room and formed its roof. When Linn burst out onto the tower porch, she looked up and saw Josie standing at the railing of the widow's walk, gazing out to sea.

Linn stopped abruptly. Her breath was coming in gasps and her legs felt trembly. She stood still, undecided what she should do. If Josie were truly considering suicide,

Linn's precipitous arrival might startle her into jumping. Should she call to Josie?

Unnoticed, Linn watched Josie for several minutes. Her back was to Linn and she stood unmoving and silent — just staring out into the bay. Suddenly she crumpled down onto the floor of the widow's walk and began to sob. Heart-rending cries were torn from Josie's lips.

Linn ran up the steep stairs and knelt beside the distraught girl. When Josie saw Linn she tried valiantly to stem her tears but could not. Linn wrapped her arms about the small figure. Wracking, groaning sobs convulsed the trembling girl's body for several moments while Linn held her and murmured soothingly to her as she would have to a heartbroken child.

Finally Josie's sobs began to subside and she disengaged herself self-consciously from Linn's arms. "I-I'm s-sorry," she mumbled as she wiped her eyes and face on the apron that she wore over her housedress.

"Don't be!" Linn said, "God meant us girls to cry, and men, too. That's why He gave us tears."

Josie covered her face with her large white apron and let out a half-sob, half-hiccup. Then she removed the apron and looked at Linn through tear-puffed eyes. "Linn, could I be excused from serving dinner? I-I need to go someplace."

"Of course, but are you all right, Josie?" Linn didn't like the idea of Josie going somewhere alone in her present state of mind.

Josie seemed to read her thoughts. "If you think I'm contemplating suicide, don't worry, I'm not. I won't say the thought hasn't entered my mind." Josie paused and looked out toward the sea. "In fact, as I was standing here I thought it would be a relief to jump off and get out of it all. But I knew I wouldn't be out of anything. I would be facing God with blood on my hands."

"Do you need my car? The keys for it are on the table by the front door."

Josie seemed about to refuse but then said gratefully, "I don't usually mind walking but it would be a big help right now. Thank you so much! And thank you for being a real friend!" She embraced Linn with a quick motion and ran down the stairs.

Linn wondered where she was going. It wasn't any of her business, she knew, but she still could not help wondering.

Linn explained to Mrs. Benholt that

Josie would not be present to help serve the evening meal. When Josie's mother frowned with annoyance, Linn told her it wouldn't be necessary for anyone to serve dinner. "I can do it. I don't mind in the least," Linn said. But Mrs. Benholt would not allow that and pressed Alfred into use.

And Alfred didn't seem to mind at all, either. In fact, he seemed to enjoy serving the table. When Linn noticed Penny's eyes dancing in glee and saw that she was having difficulty keeping a straight face, Linn began to surreptitiously watch what Alfred was doing. When he thought no one could see him, he tilted up his nose and walked with a grandiose air for all the world like a pompous butler. Then he would give Penny an exaggerated wink and she could hardly contain her giggles.

Linn couldn't resist catching Alfred's eye and giving him a wink. His face turned a fiery red. Ducking his head in embarrassment, he quickly retreated to the kitchen. Penny had caught Linn's wink, too, and saw Alfred's hasty exit. It was too much for her. She burst into almost hysterical giggles and had to excuse herself from the table until she could get them under control.

"What was that all about?" asked Clay in

astonishment. Kate looked equally mystified.

"Just a little joke between Penny and
me," Linn laughed.

About two hours after dinner, Josie returned. Clay and Linn had just come back
from a stroll along the beach in the moonlight, and were sitting on the south porch
when she drove into the garage.

Josie came up the steps and handed the
car keys to Linn with a "Thanks so much."

Linn smiled, and then asked in astonishment, "Josie, what in the world has happened to you?"

The transformation in Josie's face was
nothing short of a miracle. For a shocked
moment Linn wondered if she and Eric
were back together. Josie's face was
peaceful and joy again glowed in her soft
dark eyes.

Josie laughed softly, "I've been visiting
with my Father."

"With your father? But I thought he was
dead!" Linn exclaimed.

Josie laughed gaily, and Linn thought to
herself how good it was to hear that merry
sound from Josie again. "My heavenly Father," she explained. "I've been down at
the church talking with Him. Do you remember that I told you a while back I had

prayed and prayed but God didn't hear my prayers?"

Linn acknowledged that she did.

"Well, when I was having that cry this evening, it suddenly dawned on me that I had not really been praying, just complaining. God couldn't answer my requests because all I was doing was feeling sorry for myself and demanding that God bring Eric back to me."

A flash of pain crossed her face. "I love Eric, but God has taken the bitterness away and now I can begin living again. And this time I can truthfully say I am willing to accept whatever God has for me. And I know it will be good, even without Eric, because God is now in charge of my life."

Tears filled Linn's eyes and a joy too big to express with words rose up in her. She jumped up and hugged Josie. Hugging both girls, Clay's voice was husky as he quoted reverently, " 'My God, how great thou art!' "

21

During the following week, Clay became increasingly concerned about Eric. "Eric has been an hour late for work twice this week and when he does arrive, he looks like something the cats dragged in," Clay told Linn. "His eyes are bloodshot and he's getting almost no sleep. He must be partying every night. He's almost worthless on the job. I don't dare entrust him with the jobs he usually handles."

Linn reminded Clay that they had to leave Eric in God's hands; just as she reminded herself of the same thing. The pain in their hearts was like a deep, physical wound as they saw Eric slipping farther and farther away from God and deeper and deeper into degradation. They knew there was nothing they could do to stop his headlong descent. They could only continue to cling to God's superior power to do for Eric what they could not.

Clay said he caught glimpses of Sylvia, Eric's redheaded girlfriend, and her powerful, expensive convertible. "She doesn't even let Eric alone during the day," Clay said in disgust one night. "She comes sweeping into the parking lot in that fancy automobile and toots for him. And he goes dashing out so fast he almost runs over anyone who gets in his way. He's acting for all the world like a moonstruck teenager!"

"He still doesn't talk to you?"

"Not at all! And it isn't just this wild crowd he's running with that bothers me. He has run around with a jet-set crowd before. He and I both used to. But he just isn't himself. I would like to ask him what's happening to him but I don't dare. He's completely shut me out. I just can't understand it. I've never tried to run his life and he knows it. So why should he suddenly act like I'm trying to now? He just rushes off every evening like demons are after him."

But at least Josie was no longer a cause for concern. She went about her duties with a serene look about her. Even Joe eyed her with a puzzled expression on his face. There were days, she confided to Linn, when she had to "lean heavily upon the Lord" but that she was coming out on top there was no doubt!

Also, a new confidence was growing in Josie, a sense of her own worth. Joe could no longer intimidate her. The subservient Josie was no more.

One day Josie came to Linn and told her with a chuckle that she had gone to Joe, looked him right in the eye, and told him calmly but firmly that she wanted half of the money in their joint savings account.

"Of course he refused me with that same song and dance of 'I know what is best for us both and I will only relinquish it if you come to your senses and do what you should.' I didn't argue with him," Josie said. "I just told him plainly that half of that money was mine and if he kept it he was a thief.

"That set him back on his heels," Josie continued. "But he quickly recovered and began to lambast me for being such an utter lunatic as to fall for someone who didn't care for me. Oddly, I didn't even get upset. I just told him that being in love was as natural as breathing for a young woman."

She shook her head in astonishment. "I'm amazed at what's happening to me," Josie said in awe. "I could never stand up to Joe before. I wilted if he said so much as a cross word to me."

Linn smiled fondly at Josie. "I expect those talks with your Father have a lot to do with it."

Josie agreed. "I'm sure of it!"

The next afternoon Josie came running down the hall to Linn's room and announced in an excited voice, "Joe gave me half the money from our savings account! Not very graciously — but nevertheless I now have that money to add to the little account I started a while back. It looks like I'll be able to start school after all!"

Linn told Clay about her conversation with Josie just before bed that evening and they talked late into the night about the miraculous change they had seen in Josie. But even their joy at that couldn't mask their concern over Eric who had made a rare appearance at dinner that night.

"I'm worried, Linn," Clay told her. "I was planning on leaving Eric in charge of the business here when we returned to Grey Oaks, but with him in such an unstable condition, I can't do that. He isn't dependable anymore and he's so fractious no one can even talk to him. He's my friend and I'd never fire him, but neither do I know what to do to help him."

Linn's expressive green eyes looked at Clay with deep love and trust. "I know you care about Eric. I do, too. But we've committed him to the Lord. We can't do anything else. Only God knows what it will take to bring Eric to Him."

A troubled look creased Clay's face as he nodded. "I know. I'm just worried about what drastic measures it might take to bring Eric to the Lord." Clay smiled ruefully at Linn. "I remember what it took for the Lord to get our attention."

Linn squeezed his hand gently. She, too, remembered the pain and the struggles. A yawn escaped her as she said, "I know. But God's in control, Clay. Something will happen." Giving him a quick good night kiss, she rolled over and dropped off quickly to sleep.

Still troubled and knowing he wouldn't be able to sleep right away, Clay quietly let himself out through the French doors onto the porch. He knew it was late, but tonight there weren't any stars. Dark clouds boiled up across the far horizon and he could feel the rising wind. Standing there letting it refresh him and blow the cobwebs of doubt and frustration from him, he suddenly stiffened. He had heard something.

Not moving a muscle and straining his ears to hear, Clay stood for several long minutes. But he heard nothing more.

Putting it down to the wind and the higher surf, he turned toward the French doors. But another muffled noise reached him. The first time he had thought it came from somewhere inside the house, but now it seemed to come from outside.

Softly Clay retraced his steps to the porch railing and looked down. His eyes strained into the shadows. At first he saw nothing. Then, directly below the porch in their small, private canal, he detected a dark, moving object gliding silently toward the mouth of the channel! The shadows of the canal made it difficult to see much, but it looked like a small boat. Clay heard the whisper of an oar dipping carefully into the water. Hardly able to believe his eyes, he watched the form slip away into the darkness.

This must be the same boat Linn had seen! What was going on here?

Suddenly Clay sprang into action. Taking a strong flashlight from his room, he quickly descended the stairs to the boat garage. Flashing the powerful light about, he could see that all the Moonshell boats were still there.

Bewildered, he walked slowly along the concrete dock where the boats were floating. When the flashlight beam reached the door linking the boathouse to the canal, he saw that it was wide open. And Joe had assured him it was kept locked!

Clay felt goose bumps rise on his arms. Turning slowly back toward the inside stairway, he caught a glimpse of movement on the stairs. With quick strides he reached the bottom of the stairway and shone his light up the steps. Joe Benholt stood halfway up the stairs, shielding his eyes from the powerful beam.

Suspiciously Clay demanded, "What are you doing down here?"

"Probably the same thing you're doing. Investigating a noise," Joe said dryly.

Clay shifted the flashlight beam and Joe came down to the floor of the boathouse.

"What kind of noise did you hear?"

"I'm not sure, but it sounded like footsteps down here," Joe replied. "What sort of noise did you hear?"

"I was out on our balcony and heard a muffled sound. When I looked down, I saw a small boat in the canal heading for the bay. I came down here and found that door over there wide open again. What's going on here, Joe?"

"I wish I knew! I know you probably think I'm involved in some kind of shady operation, but I swear I don't know any more about this than you do."

"Did you know that Moonshell is being watched from boats in the bay?" asked Clay.

Joe looked surprised. "What makes you think so?"

"My wife began to notice the same green and silver boat out in the bay every day. One day she was in the tower with her binoculars and watched the man in the boat. Periodically, the fisherman would lay his fishing rod down and scan the house with his own glasses. Sometimes the same man — a big guy with red hair and a beard — uses a small sailboat instead of the motorboat. But he's definitely watching the house."

Joe digested this bit of news. After a minute or two he asked, "You people aren't in some kind of trouble with the law, are you? I don't ever recall hearing noises in the boathouse before. And why should anyone be watching Moonshell? This whole business is downright eerie."

Clay laughed. "We're completely lawabiding, I assure you. We're absolutely mystified about everything that's been happening here. We don't have any enemies that I know of — unless it would be my former fiance, Bonnie Leeds. At one time she had a grudge against my wife — and probably me, too — because I married Linn instead of her. But that was a long time ago."

"Where does this woman live?"

"Idaho," Clay responded. "But she is in Corpus Christi right now."

"Maybe she's your culprit," Joe said thoughtfully.

Clay laughed again. "She's a dainty little socialite. It would be hard to imagine her soiling her hands with poison or pushing people off porches."

Joe didn't laugh. "If she has money, she wouldn't have to do her own dirty work."

Staring hard at Joe, Clay's eyes searched his face as if looking for answers there. Without a word, though, he turned and led the way upstairs.

Could it be possible? The idea of Bonnie actually trying to do real bodily harm to Linn — or anyone — seemed preposterous. But was it just coincidence that she had appeared here in Corpus Christi so far from home?

22

The next morning Clay had made up his mind. Before he left for work with Eric, he told Linn that he wanted her, Kate and Penny to start packing.

Disappointed and distressed, Linn tried to talk him out of it. "I'd miss you terribly, Clay. Couldn't we just move over to Corpus Christi into a house or apartment?"

"I'd like you with me, too, Linn, but I told you what happened last night. I should have sent you home immediately after that episode with Baby. Every moment I let you stay here, I'm putting your life in jeopardy. I think you'll be safer at home. We don't know why this person wants to harm you. There are midnight prowlers apparently roaming freely in and about the grounds — maybe even in the house for all we know. No. It's time for you to leave."

"But nothing has ever happened except at Moonshell. And nothing has ever happened when anyone else was around," Linn reasoned.

Clay paused, considering her words. Then he grinned his crooked grin. "All right. You win. Truthfully, the thought of you being clear off in Idaho for the rest of the summer doesn't sound very appealing. We'll take a house or nice apartment over in Corpus Christi for the rest of the summer. But at the first hint of danger, back to Idaho you go. No more arguments. To be honest, I don't like leaving you at Moonshell even to pack."

"I'm sure I'll be all right. Penny will be with me."

"Kate will be with you, too," Clay said emphatically. "I want someone with you every minute while you are at Moonshell. We can spare Kate at the office so she and Penny can be with you at all times. Nothing has ever happened when someone else is present. You should be safe. You three get Josie — and Mrs. Benholt and the maids, too, if you need them — to help you get our things packed. I'll check on a house or apartment today. If I don't find one right away, we can move to a hotel until we do. But I want you out of here today."

"Okay," Linn said. She would have agreed to almost anything to keep from being separated from Clay for the rest of the summer. "Clay! I just thought of something! What about Josie? If we don't take her with us, she'll be out of a job."

"Bring her along. We'll need someone in our new place. I'll also be responsible for Joe's and Mrs. Benholt's salaries until I contact Clyde Cameron."

That evening Linn told Clay everything was packed and ready to go. Clay had looked at a large house in town which seemed ideal, but had not been able to contact the owner who was out of town for the day. "If you'll be real careful for another day. I'll see him tomorrow," Clay told her. "His daughter showed me the house but she doesn't take care of the renting."

But the next morning when Linn went downstairs to have breakfast with Clay before he went to work, she noticed a worried expression on his face. A strong, gale-like wind was blowing and heavy dark clouds scuttled across the murky sky. The bay looked choppy and grey.

When Mrs. Benholt brought their breakfast in to them, she asked if they had heard the weather forecast. When they said that they hadn't, she informed them that the hurricane which had been brewing off the coast was moving toward land. "We could be in for some rough weather," she added. "I know you all aren't used to hurricane country so I thought I better warn you to keep up on the news. It could come ashore at any time today unless it veers off."

"What happens if the hurricane comes ashore?" Linn asked with some trepidation.

"We tie everything down the best we can and go inland until it's over," Mrs. Benholt answered.

Josie entered just then with a platter of toast and a pot of hot chocolate. "It can be fun," she said. "We always take camping gear and stay at an out-of-the-way camp we know about."

Penny was listening to all of this with wide-eyed eagerness. Now, her eyes bright with anticipation, she interposed, "Couldn't we camp out, too?"

Clay grinned. "You had better ask your mother and Linn if they want to make like Davy Crockett!"

"Why not?" Kate smiled. "What do you say, Linn?"

"Sounds like a fun adventure to me," she agreed.

"When do we leave?" Penny asked excitedly.

Eric, who had stopped to listen before dashing out the door, spoke up, "Hey! Whoa! We don't know for sure we're getting a hurricane yet." He glanced enigmatically at Clay before he turned to Mrs. Benholt. "Would you object to our following you to the campground you mentioned if we do have to run from the hurricane?"

"Certainly not. And you wouldn't need to buy tents or anything. Mr. Cameron and his family were always prepared for anything. There are plenty in the basement."

Later that day, Linn went for a walk down the beach. She knew she shouldn't go alone but having someone with her constantly was telling on her nerves, not to mention the tension of waiting on the approaching storm. The beach appeared to be deserted and there was only the motorboat out in the bay.

She walked slowly along the wet sand, just at the edge of the water, mulling over Eric's strange actions and almost reluctant concern. His dark, haggard face worried her. Would he be there to help if they needed him today? A wave boiled around Linn's feet, breaking into her thoughts.

She welcomed the sensation. Stooping down, she picked up a shell the waves had washed in. Most were broken or chipped but this one was a perfect, snow white moon shell. As she stood turning it over and over in her hand, she let her brooding gaze drift toward the magnificent mansion. It never ceased to amaze her how the architect had so skillfully designed the building to resemble a milky white moon shell.

"And to think," she mused softly, aloud, "this pure white, innocent-looking shell houses a creature capable of capturing and devouring a shellfish." She shuddered. "I'm getting morbid," she told herself. "As far as I'm concerned this is just a pretty shell to add to our collection!"

She glanced again at Moonshell. *So beautiful — but like the note said, moon shells are vicious killers. And a killer prowls at will inside this Moonshell, playing a deadly cat and mouse game with me! Who? Why?*

She shivered. The gloomy weather must be affecting her usual optimism.

She turned and walked on down the beach. But her apprehensions had spoiled her day. She stopped to watch a graceful tern plummet into the bay like a white bullet, and come up with a small silvery fish wriggling in his orange bill. Perched on a large piece of driftwood, his black cap glistening against the snowy white of his breast and back, he gulped down his catch.

"He's pretty enough to paint," she murmured, "but he's a killer, too."

Linn looked out in the bay and saw the motorboat bobbing in the rising waves. Suddenly she was angry — angry at being spied on and angry at the threats.

She threw the moon shell down on the hard-packed, wet sand and stamped it into tiny white bits. But even as the last fragment disintegrated, a Scripture she had read that morning in the Psalms popped into her mind. *When I cry out to You, then my enemies will turn back; this I know, because God is for me.*

The verse stopped her. *If God is on our side, we don't need to fear anything,* she thought, relieved and ashamed of her outburst a few moments ago. With a lighter heart, she turned back toward Moonshell.

As she neared the house, Kate came hurrying down the path to meet her. "I couldn't find you and I was getting worried," she said.

"I'm sorry," Linn apologized. "I went a little farther down the beach than I intended to. I was getting a little stir crazy from being in the house so much. I'm sorry if I worried you."

After lunch she told Kate and Penny that she felt a little tired and was going up to take a nap.

"Josie wants to clean yours and Eric's rooms this afternoon. Since she will be just down the hall from our rooms, and I'm going to be resting anyway, why don't you two do whatever you want for a couple of hours?"

"All right," Kate agreed, "if you promise to leave your door wide open."

Linn smiled and agreed. When asked, Josie quickly consented to check on Linn and to come immediately if Linn should call. So Kate and Penny went away and Linn settled down on her comfortable waterbed for a nap.

Suddenly all the lights went out and she was walking down the hall of Moonshell, groping — groping to find her way. She heard a sound and turned. Close behind her was an enormous, glistening white moon shell! She was petrified with fear. She tried to run, but seemed glued to the spot.

To her horror, she saw a huge black foot slide out of the shell and begin to inch toward her. She could not move — nor speak

— as the slimy, black foot came closer and closer and closer. Just as the horrible thing reached out to grab her Linn was finally able to scream. And scream she did! Loud and long! And her own scream awoke her!

Drenched with perspiration, Linn sat up. Her eyes darted about the room fearfully. The door that had been left wide open was still wide open and she was still alone. But the haunting dream was so real, she almost felt like looking under the bed to see if that dreadful creature was lurking there!

Suddenly Josie came tearing into the room. When she saw Linn sitting up in bed, she came rushing over. "Are you all right? What happened?"

Before Linn could answer, the housekeeper, Kate and Penny were all there, everyone asking questions at one time.

Linn laughed shakily, "I'm sorry. I just had a nightmare. But it was so real — and horrible." She shuddered at the memory.

That night when Clay came home and heard about the dream, he looked grim. "This place is getting to you. I still didn't get to see that fellow about the house but I'm getting you away from here. We'll go to a hotel — tomorrow!"

23

But when they awoke the next morning, a heavy wind was battering the house. Clay switched on the radio. The announcer was warning all the residents of the coastal towns to batten down everything and flee inland. The hurricane was almost certain to reach the Rockport area within the next twenty-four hours. The emergency message reported the hurricane to be the worst of the decade. Damage was expected to be extremely heavy.

The plans to move into a hotel in Corpus Christi were immediately abandoned as they prepared to evacuate inland until the hurricane passed. Everyone agreed it was best to keep the luggage to a minimum, taking only the essentials. They would have to risk that the house and its contents would still be intact after the hurricane had blown itself out. But Moonshell had been built to withstand storms, and it had weathered hurricanes before.

Making a rare appearance at breakfast, Eric was grimly silent while Kate mourned that here they were, all packed to move, and now they must dig into everything to get what was really needed for the next few days. The others agreed it was unfortunate, but no one wasted a lot of time in regrets. There was too much to do.

Linn helped Kate and Penny pack theirs and Eric's things while the two men gathered camping gear from the basement and loaded it into the family station wagon and Eric's car. They also helped Joe install heavy shutters on the windows and put lawn furniture and other objects likely to blow away into the garage and storage rooms.

Just after noon Kate, Penny, Eric and Clay left to go into town. They had to close up the office and remove their most important papers. With a quick hug, Clay left Linn and the Benholts to finish at Moonshell.

Josie had packed her suitcase the night before, halfway expecting that they would have to move inland today. She and Linn were going in Linn's little Volkswagen. Joe had marked the route he usually took on the map for Linn but Josie also knew the way. They all had agreed to meet at the campground as soon as everyone could get there.

"Remember," Joe said, "if we get separated, stay off the main highways as much as possible. Take the farm-to-market roads and other side roads going in the right direction. The hundred mile trip may take all day because of the heavy exodus of cars going inland."

Joe put Linn's, Clay's and Josie's suitcases in Linn's car. The Benholt suitcases and camping gear were already packed into Joe's car. They all went back for one last check of the house and then returned to their cars. Mrs. Benholt and Alfred were riding with Joe.

Linn was certain she had left her purse lying in the seat of the Volks but when she reached for it to get out her car keys, it wasn't there. "I must have left my purse in my room," she told Josie. "I'll run back and get it."

"I'll go with you," offered Josie.

"There's no need," Linn said. "I'll be right back."

Linn called to Joe who was sitting behind the steering wheel of his car, ready to leave, "You go on ahead since you have to fill up with gas. There could be a long line at the gas station. If I don't catch up with you before, we'll see you at the camp-ground."

"We don't mind waiting," Joe said.

"It isn't necessary," Linn called. "I'll be back in a flash."

Linn did not see the faint flutter of the upper-story window curtain as she raced back into the house.

I'm glad I put on sensible, rubber-soled shoes and jeans with all this running back and forth, she thought, dashing up the stairs and down the hall to her room. The purse wasn't on her bed. She stood in the middle of the room and looked around. The purse was nowhere to be seen.

Perhaps I left it in the study. With a few quick strides she was standing at the door. Just as she spied the purse lying on a corner of the desk, she heard a sound in the bedroom. *Josie must have followed me up after all,* she thought as she retrieved her purse and walked quickly back into her bedroom.

She felt her blood turn to ice water.

A swarthy-skinned, black-bearded Mexican man stood in the middle of her bedroom!

For a moment Linn was too shocked and frightened to speak. Then, praying silently for help, Linn tried to still the panic that threatened to engulf her. She would have made a mad dash for the hall but the intruder stood between her and the doorway.

"What are you doing in my house?" Linn tried to keep the tremble from her voice by speaking loudly.

Unsmiling the Mexican spoke in a surly, commanding voice, "The senora will come with me."

Before Linn could retort, Josie rushed into the room. "You were gone so long I —" Then she saw the strange, unkempt stranger. With astonishment she said, "What's going on here?"

The ruffian opened his mouth in the semblance of a smile, showing yellowed teeth with a couple missing in the lower jaw. "Well," he said in a heavily accented voice, "a senorita. Two ees better than one." The smirk disappeared. "Vamos! We go now."

"We aren't going anywhere with you!" Linn stated firmly.

A dangerous gleam appeared in the black eyes staring at her from heavy, shaggy black brows. The man's lips curled into a contemptuous sneer, "Go!" He motioned toward the corner of the room to Linn's left.

Linn glanced that way and gasped in shock. A section about the size of a door was open in the wall! As soon as Linn saw the opening, several pieces of the mystery tumbled into place. So that was how someone could come and go in her room with the doors securely locked!

Suddenly the Mexican stepped over and with a soiled hand grasped Josie by the forearm, propelling her toward the opening. With the other hand he grabbed Linn's arm just below the elbow and shoved them both ahead of him into the open section in the wall.

Linn tried to pull away, but the grip on her arm only tightened until she cried out. The Mexican relaxed his grip slightly and pushed first Linn and then Josie through the opening. He followed them in, leaned over and stuck his finger into a small notch cut into the baseboard. The wall slowly and noiselessly rolled back into place.

Linn looked about. Her heart was beating like a jackhammer but she was still curious. They were standing on a narrow landing and Linn could see stone steps leading steeply downward into a murky darkness.

Their abductor herded them downward, shining a small light on the treads. Linn and Josie clung tightly to the metal handrail as they descended into the dim, shadowy interior. The tunnel-like stairway smelled musty and damp.

At the first floor, there was a tiny landing; the stairs reversed sides and continued to descend steeply.

"This leads to the boathouse I'm sure," Josie whispered.

In the dim light they could make out a small door at the foot of the steps. Suddenly, without warning, the door burst open and the narrow passageway was flooded with brilliant light that blinded their eyes!

They could see nothing but a rough male voice drawled, "Come on down, ladies, and join the party."

"We can't see the steps unless you take that light out of our eyes," Linn said, struggling to keep her voice from quivering.

The bright light was shifted to the steps in front of them and the girls moved slowly and fearfully down until they were standing on the floor of the boat garage.

The powerful beam was shut off and Linn saw two other men in the lighted boathouse. One was a big, pot-bellied, stubble-faced hulk of a man. His sour odor reached her nostrils even though he was several feet from her. He was dressed in dirty dungarees like the Mexican who had captured them.

The other man was also a Mexican but he seemed out of place with his disreputable companions. He looked vaguely familiar but Linn could not recall where she might have seen him. He had every appearance of a gentleman. Neatly dressed in dark, expensively cut slacks, soft pink shirt, plaid sport coat, and neatly knotted black and pink tie, he could well have been an affluent businessman. He was good-looking with a small black mustache, and glistening black, carefully groomed hair.

By her side, Linn could sense that Josie had stiffened. She turned to stare at her. Josie took a step toward the suave Mexican.

"Carlos Rodriguez de la Zorro," Josie said slowly. "What are you doing here?"

The good-looking Mexican smiled, showing even, white teeth. "Miss Benholt, it is a pleasure to see you again. And this other charming lady must be Senora Randolph. I am indeed sorry that we must detain you both for a bit — until we finish our little operation here." His voice was cultured; his manner genteel.

Josie started to speak when Linn let out a startled gasp and clutched Josie's arm. Josie's eyes followed Linn's wide-eyed gaze. A section of the boathouse wall a few feet from them was open, and through the opening was a well-lighted room filled with beautiful articles of all kinds!

Entranced, Linn and Josie were drawn as by a magnet. No one made a move to stop them as they inspected the treasures more closely. They stepped into the room, which measured probably ten by ten, and saw that shelves lined all the walls. Many pieces of gold, curiously wrought figurines and silver and copper jewelry set with jade and other stones were laid out on one shelf. Strangely decorated pottery and small statues of stone, metal and clay stood on other shelves.

Linn suddenly saw something that practically took her breath away. Lying innocently in the middle of the jewelry shelf was Penny's exquisite jade and gold pendant! Like a light going on, Linn knew what these articles were!

"These are Mayan artifacts," she whispered to Josie, "treasures stolen from Mayan ruins or graves!"

"You're very perceptive, young lady. They are, indeed, priceless Mayan artifacts. But I don't like the word 'stolen.' " The Mexican gentleman had followed them into the room and had heard Linn's whispered information. He smiled. "I bought them so they are mine to dispose of in any manner I choose.

"Now, we must move outside and let these gentlemen get on with their work." He motioned the women out ahead of him. As they exited, Linn noticed a wooden box on the floor, partly packed with paper-wrapped objects. The two grubby men immediately set to work. Although they looked like bums, the laborers obviously were skilled in their work. They wrapped each piece carefully but swiftly.

"Shall we sit down?" the gentleman thief asked courteously as he produced a folding chair and two boxes from nearby.

"Who gave you permission to use Moonshell for storing your contraband?" Linn demanded.

The Mexican man raised an expressive eyebrow, "I assure you, dear lady, we not only have permission but paid a good fee for the privilege."

"To whom?" Linn asked, her ire raising. "Moonshell is ours for the summer and no one had a right to allow you to invade our privacy!"

"Linn," Josie interrupted urgently, "we need to be leaving. The hurricane is moving in."

"I know," their captor replied. "That's why we are moving out our treasures."

"Let's go," Linn told Josie as she turned toward the stairs. "Our families are going to be wondering what happened to us."

Instantly a strong brown hand grasped Linn's wrist and pulled her back. "Leaving at this time is out of the question, Senora Randolph. I'm sorry."

Linn felt chills playing tag up and down her spine. "What are you going to do with us?"

The suave smuggler smiled his gracious smile and seemed to be considering. "I'm not sure as yet, but, of course, I would not cold-bloodedly murder two such lovely ladies."

Linn didn't know whether to be relieved or not. She wondered if he was just toying with them. She had been watching his eyes. His well-chiseled lips would curve into a smile so readily but no warmth touched his dark eyes. Those glacial black eyes reminded her of the glittery, cold eyes of an octopus she had seen recently in an aquarium.

"You still haven't told me who gave you

permission to store your goods here," Linn said.

Carlos's smile turned frosty and he spoke impatiently, "I haven't and I don't plan to!" His icy eyes glittered. "Let it suffice to say that money will buy almost anything and almost anyone!"

The handsome Mexican stood up leisurely and strolled to the door of the treasure room. He spoke to the workmen in rapid Spanish. There was a brief reply in Spanish from the other Mexican.

"If you ladies will excuse me, I must assist my workmen. And, please, do not entertain thoughts of escaping." He wasn't smiling now. "I would dislike having to tie those shapely arms and feet. Bonds are extremely uncomfortable, and besides, we have no time for games."

The man took off his immaculate coat and folded it carefully before laying it over a box. He unbuttoned his shirt cuffs and turned them back three folds before he began helping to remove artifacts from the shelves and rapidly pack them into the waiting boxes. Linn noticed his hands were soft and smooth like someone who did not often indulge in physical labor.

Linn looked about, but saw no strange boat in their boathouse. She wondered how the men had come. She half-expected to see the dark boat she had seen gliding into and out of their canal the nights she had awakened. How were they going to transport the packed treasures away from Moonshell?

She soon found out!

As soon as the artifacts were all in boxes and securely tied, the three men began to load them into the Moonshell yacht.

Linn jumped to her feet and protested, "You can't do that! That yacht belongs to Clyde Cameron!"

The handsome smuggler carefully set his burden down in the bottom of the yacht before he climbed out of the boat and answered Linn.

"Can't? That's a strong word to use with me, young lady." His face mirrored amusement. Suddenly his hand shot out and grasped Linn's arm. It was deceptively hard and strong. His voice was soft, "You're in no position to tell me what I cannot do." He sneered at her. "Never get Carlos de la Zorro angry, Senora! It is dangerous!"

24

It took the smugglers about an hour to carefully wrap, pack and load the Mayan artifacts. They completely ignored Linn and Josie while they worked.

Watching them, Linn wondered how long the thieves had been storing treasures at Moonshell but she decided it would not be wise to ask questions. Perhaps if she and Josie were docile and quiet, the men would set them free when they left. Of one thing she was certain, she didn't wish to anger the gentlemanly Carlos. He frightened her.

When the storeroom was empty and every box had been stowed in the yacht, Linn heard the big Anglo ask Carlos, "Whatcha goin' to do wit' them?" Carlos didn't answer, but he came down out of the boat and stood staring at the two women.

Carlos wasn't smiling now. Perhaps he

had tired of his little charade. A quiver began in Linn's stomach as she noticed how thin and merciless Carlos's mouth appeared without a smile. A petition surged up from deep inside her, *"God help us."*

"I know you ladies have been wondering why Juan sneaked that purse out of your car so you would have to come back in and get it." He smiled his bleak smile. "Not just to have your company I assure you, though that is not unpleasant, but we needed a hostage — or two. It will be helpful to have you along in case anyone questions our possession of the Moonshell yacht."

Linn was aghast, "You surely don't mean you are taking us with you. We won't go! You can't. . . ."

"We can't what?" Carlos's lips had thinned to a hard, cruel line. His voice was harsh and threatening. "We can do whatever we wish to do! Who's to stop us?" He laughed unpleasantly. "Your men must think very little of you anyway to run off and leave you to shift for yourselves. Now, I have very little patience so please do as I say! Get in the boat!"

Linn and Josie moved to do his bidding. Neither he nor the other two men offered to help the girls into the streamlined yacht, but left them to scramble over the side the best way they could. Then Carlos sprang over the side with the agility of an athlete.

Linn wished fervently that she hadn't sent Joe on ahead. But what if Joe had waited? She suddenly knew with clarity that they would have just been captured, too, and possibly been left tied up in the house — or dumped in the Gulf. Linn shivered.

Carlos took his place at the wheel before he gave his orders in a terse voice, "Juan, take the senora into the cabin and keep her quiet. Frank, after you open and close the garage door, you go into the cabin, too. If that woman makes a sound, slug her." His dark, smoldering eyes bored into Linn's as he gave the order.

Linn's knees went weak. Her body felt chilled and clammy with fear. What was this evil man going to do with them? If only Clay were here! But he was many miles away with no idea she was in trouble. She and Josie were alone with this merciless bandit. Josie! What plans did Carlos have for her? She hadn't been ordered into the cabin.

Juan laid hold of Linn's arm with a rough, stained hand and steered her toward the cabin. She looked back at Josie and saw that she was standing near

Carlos's side with her back to Linn. Linn couldn't hear the soft words that Carlos was speaking to Josie but she saw that he was smiling again.

Juan pulled Linn into the cabin and pushed her roughly into the padded seat at the table. Then he went to draw the cabin drapes, but Linn hardly noticed. A new thought — wild and incredible surely — had surfaced in Linn's mind. Was Josie Carlos's accomplice? Had she given him a key to the Moonshell boathouse?

The idea was absurd! They had trusted Josie completely. Linn felt like she was spinning in a whirlpool so mixed up were her thoughts. Surely Josie was not mixed up in this smuggling plot. Surely not!

But stark, frightening facts loomed out of the confusion in her mind. Linn had left Josie in the car, but it had been only a few minutes from the time Linn arrived in the Randolph bedroom when Josie appeared.

And Carlos was not treating Josie the same as he was treating Linn. The last she had seen of Josie on deck, Carlos was smiling at her very companionably! Was she somehow connected with this suave, Mexican smuggler?

If Josie was truly accepting money from these smugglers and throwing Moonshell open to dangerous outlaws, there wasn't anything she wouldn't do for money! It was almost more than Linn could imagine but she had to examine the facts.

And someone had tried to murder Linn — twice! It would have been easy for Josie to be that person. She lived at Moonshell and had ready access to the whole place. She knew where Linn would be at any given time. But it couldn't be! Not sweet, gentle Josie!

Linn's head was swirling but she forced herself to probe deeper. Josie knew Carlos; she had acknowledged that she did. Could innocent-appearing Josie and the dashing, handsome brigand be sweethearts? Linn felt betrayed and nauseous at the thought.

But Josie was a Christian! Or was she? Maybe Josie had been pretending all along and was just a superb actress? People were not always what they seemed. Linn felt sick. Surely she was jumping to a lot of un-substantiated conclusions.

But more suspicious acts paraded relent-lessly through Linn's mind. Why did Carlos send Linn to the cabin and keep Josie out on the deck? To be near her? What had he been saying to her a couple of minutes ago that was apparently meant just for Josie's ears?

Linn's painful meditations and questions were interrupted by the sound of the powerful yacht motor starting. She heard the throb of the engine and the swish and splash of water as the boat moved out of the boat garage into the canal. The grating of the closing garage door fell harshly on her jittery nerves. Then the big, pot-bellied Anglo entered the cabin and Linn wondered if she could stand the stench of his filthy body in the confined quarters.

Thankfully, the man called Frank moved on past her and stood peeking out around the edge of the porthole curtain. The boat moved smoothly down the channel. Suddenly, Linn felt the boat begin to rock and she knew they were coming out into the bay where the storm was stirring the water into choppy waves.

Frank turned his small, beady, bloodshot eyes toward Linn and snarled in a raspy voice, "Ya heard the boss! No funny stuff or I'll make a punchin' bag outa ya!"

Linn kept her eyes averted and didn't answer.

Suddenly Linn heard a shout and her heart lurched, beginning to pound with hope. Was it the man in the silver and green boat? Linn recalled that he had been there early this morning, bouncing and bobbing in the waves.

The call came again and Linn's keen ears picked up the words, "Hey there, friends, it's dangerous to be out in a boat today. A hurricane is blowing in."

After a moment Josie's voice called back. "We know. We are just moving the yacht over to Copano Bay where it should be safer."

"You'd better get that boat parked and move inland as soon as possible," the male voice shouted.

"Thank you, we are," Josie replied in a loud and cheerful voice.

The stranger's voice didn't come again. Linn felt bitter despair and fear boiling up inside her, threatening to choke her. She had never felt so alone in all of her twenty-five years. She was shut into a fragile yacht with three dangerous outlaws and bouncing around in the bay with a hurricane bearing down upon them. One thing she was thankful for, she had not been nauseous this morning. She must not even think about it now, though, lest the power of suggestion get it stirred up.

Another shattering thought pressed its way into her mind. If anything happened to her, the baby that she was carrying would also die. She and Clay would never know the joy of holding their own tiny baby in their arms!

Angrily, Linn told herself that God was still God and she was His child! *Now, cut out the foolishness and exercise some faith for the good and not the bad,* she scolded herself. *Oh God, please help me,* she cried out silently. And even though she was still a prisoner and the hurricane was still charging down upon them, she felt better. She had shifted her fears to the hefty shoulders of the Lord.

25

Clay and Eric with Kate and Penny arrived at the Clawson Campground around midnight. They had battled bumper-to-bumper traffic on the major highways and even the smaller roads. It seemed the whole world was moving inland.

The large campground was in an out-of-the-way location, but it was still almost full. Clay drove through the camp with Eric following in his car, looking for Linn and the Benholts. They finally located the Benholt automobile and tent, but there was no sign of Linn's little Volkswagen.

Kate and Penny waited in the cars while Clay and Eric stiffly climbed out and went over to the Benholt tent. A light was on and when Clay called, Joe opened the tent door almost instantly. He was fully dressed, as were Alfred and Mrs. Benholt who crowded in behind him.

Joe looked disappointed when he saw

Clay and Eric. "I thought you would be Josie and Mrs. Randolph," Joe said. "We've been here almost two hours and they still haven't arrived."

Quick alarm registered in Clay's face. "You got separated from them?"

Joe's expression was apologetic. "I did a stupid thing. Mrs. Randolph had to go back in the house for her purse and she insisted on us going on since I had to get gas and she didn't. There was a long line and it took us quite a while to get the tank filled. I presumed Mrs. Randolph had gone on ahead because the last thing she said was 'If we get separated from each other, we'll see you at the campground.'"

Joe's face looked strained. "I'm sorry, Mr. Randolph. I should have checked on them before I left town. I'm sure they'll be in soon but it does worry a person."

Clay's face clouded with deep concern. He turned to Eric, "We'd better go back and check on them, don't you think?"

"Yes," Eric said. "Those girls could have had engine trouble, gotten lost, or anything. It shouldn't take us as long to go back. Most of the traffic will be coming out instead of going in."

"Josie knows the way well so they couldn't have gotten lost," Joe reasoned. "I still believe they'll show up any minute now. Why don't you all come in and have some of Mom's freshly made coffee and rolls? Then we'll set up your tents, so Mrs. Marshall and Penny can get some rest. That'll give Mrs. Randolph and Josie a little more time to get in. If they aren't here by that time, I'll go back with you to find them."

"One of us men should stay here," Eric said. "I should go back with Clay, so why don't you stay with the camp, Joe?"

Joe's hair-trigger temper flared. "My sister is back there so I want to go!"

A shadow of the old Eric flared up as he shot back, "You should have thought about that when you ran off and left them!"

Joe's face flushed fiery red and his eyes glinted with anger. "It wasn't my idea! Mrs. Randolph told me to go!"

Clay stepped between them. "Hey, you guys! Everyone's nerves are frayed. It won't help if we get to fighting among ourselves. Let's bring Kate and Penny inside and then get those tents up."

In the end it was Eric who went with Clay about forty-five minutes later. Mrs. Benholt convinced Joe to stay in camp.

26

As the yacht moved out into Aransas Bay late in the afternoon, the wind became stronger and the waves higher and rougher. Swells rolling in caused the ship to toss violently. The farther they went, the rougher the water became and Linn wondered uneasily how close the hurricane was.

Frank went out on deck, to Linn's profound relief, as soon as they were a good distance from the Moonshell dock. Juan stayed in the cabin and under his surly, watchful eyes, Linn dared not leave her seat.

An hour or so later Linn noticed a change in the sound of the motor and the movement of the boat. She realized they must be rounding the point of land and entering the channel that led into Copano Bay. The wind was still brisk and the swells still rolled but not as strongly as out in the more open Aransas Bay.

Linn thought, *if the water is this rough in*

Aransas and Copano Bays, I wonder what it is like out in the Gulf of Mexico? She shuddered and was thankful for San Juan and the other islands which created some protection for the Rockport area from the full blast of the approaching storm.

A while later Linn heard the yacht motor begin to cut back and knew they must be coming into a dock somewhere. Soon the engine was just a gentle throb. Linn heard the bumping and felt the jar as the boat nudged into the sides of the dock and then stopped.

Frank stuck his head in the door of the cabin and addressed Juan. "The boss said to tie the girl's hands and come on out and help us unload — and to be quick about it."

Juan grunted an affirmative. Quickly locating some rope in a cupboard, he tied Linn's hands behind her. When he drew the rope so tight she winced, he slacked it off but it was still uncomfortably tight. She knew that if she were tied long, her hands would soon be throbbing.

Linn's heart was pounding so hard, she wondered if Juan had heard it booming as he left the cabin. What was going to happen to her? It was maddening to be shut up like this. If she could only see what was going on, it would help.

The sounds of hurrying footsteps, the sliding of boxes and the grunts of the men as they hefted their loads, came clearly to her sharp ears. Every sound spoke of haste. She wondered if Josie was helping unload some of the smaller boxes.

Suddenly Linn heard Frank's raspy voice exclaim, "Boss, a car's comin' down the beach road and it's comin' fast!"

There was a pause and then Carlos spoke in an urgent tone, "Juan, go inside and tie something over that girl's mouth and stay with her unless we need you. Get your gun ready in case it's the cops. I don't plan to lose these artifacts!"

Linn heard Juan's quick footsteps headed for the cabin door. Then she heard Carlos's voice again. "Frank, just take it easy. Act like we are just moving some things out of the hurricane area."

Juan came into the cabin and began to rummage in a drawer. Then Linn heard Carlos say, "Josie —" But his voice was low and Linn couldn't hear the rest above the shuffling of Juan's feet and the sound of the opening and closing drawers. But, reluctantly, it registered with Linn that the smuggler no longer used the polite "Miss Benholt." It was now the more intimate "Josie."

Was Josie a part of this smuggling operation or even Carlos's girlfriend? Or was she, like Linn, involved strictly by accident? If only she knew, one way or the other.

Linn's musings were interrupted by Juan tying a heavy piece of cloth over her mouth. She glared at him and he stood back and smirked. "Lady," he said in a heavily accented voice, "if you make even the little sound, Juan push rag inside your mouth. Sabe?"

Linn's eyes held his for a long moment, and then she heard the sound of a powerful motor, the crunch of tires on gravel and car doors slamming. Hope surged in her heart. Was help coming?

"Hi there!" a youngish male voice called amiably. "Moving some things, are you?"

"Si, Senor," Carlos's smooth voice sounded friendly. "As soon as we get these few things loaded into my pick-up, we are getting out of here. I would advise you to do the same, my friends."

"Can we help?" another male voice inquired.

"Muchos gracias, mi amigos, but there is no need. We are almost finished."

"Say," the first voice said, "would you mind if I looked in the cabin of your yacht? I'm thinking of buying one and whenever I see a different one, I look it over so's to get an idea of what I want."

Linn thought she detected a testiness in Carlos's voice, but he answered pleasantly enough. "I'm sorry, but a friend is sick and he's asleep in there right now."

"I'm afraid we'll have to insist," the first stranger's voice said, authority ringing in it. "We're police officers."

"Well," Carlos's voice was as smooth as polished marble, "I don't know what you hope to find, but help yourself. Please do not disturb my friend."

Linn saw that Juan had come to his feet and was listening tensely. A wicked looking gun had appeared in his soiled fist.

Linn felt the motion of the ship as the two men came aboard. Low, indistinguishable commands and scuffing noises came to Linn's ears. Then footsteps approached the cabin door.

Fear gorged in Linn's throat. Juan was crouched just beyond the door, pistol in readiness. The policemen were walking into a trap! Linn knew that she, too, was in a very precarious position so near the door. But if she tried to warn the policemen or even tried to move to a safer place, Juan would probably shoot her!

The steps had stopped at the door. Linn

tensed as she saw the door begin to open. "Watch out!" She forced the words through the rag tied over her mouth with all her might.

She glimpsed Juan's fiercely angry glare as he half-spun and leveled the gun at her. Desperately, she threw herself down in the padded seat a second before she heard the reverberating crack of Juan's pistol and the whistle of the bullet as it passed over her body, piercing the back of the seat.

Expecting the next bullet to smash into her body, Linn rolled off the bench onto the floor. She lay semi-stunned from the impact as her whole left side and head hit the floor with a dull thud. Another shot quickly followed the first. Linn dimly heard a cry, and then a string of violently angry Spanish words.

"Are you all right, ma'am?" A curly-haired young man peered under the table at Linn. One square, tanned hand held a police revolver, but it was pointed away from Linn.

"I-I think so," Linn mumbled through the cloth over her mouth.

Reaching over with one hand, the man pulled the rag from Linn's mouth and she took a deep breath. With the help of the curly-haired man, who kept his gun trained on Juan while he helped Linn out with the other hand, she rolled and scooted her way from under the table.

Linn's head hurt from the jar of hitting the floor and her shoulder and hip felt bruised, but she had never cherished the sensation more. She was alive! A moment ago she wouldn't have given a peso for her chances.

"I'm Ted Guffrey," the young policeman told Linn. "My partner is Officer Jim Bowers."

"I'm Linn Randolph. These men kidnapped me a while ago from Moonshell. They're smugglers."

"I know," the young policeman said.

She preceded Juan and Officer Guffrey out onto the darkened deck. A tall, tough-looking, middle-aged man was holding a gun on Carlos and Frank who were lying spread-eagled on the deck. The younger policeman ordered Juan to join them.

"What you mean, man?" he sputtered, "I'm bleeding." And he was. Juan's left hand was curled tightly around his right wrist and blood was dripping onto the deck from between his fingers.

Police Officer Bowers pulled a large handkerchief from his pocket and tossed it to Juan. "Tie that around your arm and then get down there with the others," he commanded.

Muttering in Spanish and looking venomously at the officer, Juan did as he was told.

Linn thought the policemen were cruel until a minute later when the young officer searched the men. He pulled a wicked looking razor from Juan's pocket and more weapons from the other two men's clothing. Carlos had a knife in a scabbard inside one polished field boot.

Josie was backed up against the side of the cabin when Linn, Juan and Officer Guffrey appeared on deck. Now she moved toward Linn but the older police officer spoke sharply, "Stay right where you are, sister!"

Linn saw Josie turn shocked eyes toward the officer. "You — You don't think I'm one of t-them, do you?" When he hesitated, she turned imploring dark eyes to Linn. "Linn, tell him I'm not one of the smugglers!"

Total confusion reigned in Linn's mind. She wanted to assure the policemen that Josie was innocent, but she honestly didn't know herself. She opened her mouth but nothing came out. She just didn't know what to say!

27

The decision was taken from her when Carlos spoke scornfully from his prone position on the deck. "What's the matter, Senorita Benholt? Don't you want anyone to know you have dealings with dirty old smugglers?"

"I didn't!" Josie turned soft, distressed eyes upon the officers. "He's not telling the truth!"

"I'm sorry, Miss," the younger officer said as he clamped handcuffs on her slim wrists.

Linn was grateful when the curly-haired officer untied her arms so she could turn her attention away from Josie. Her hands were half-numb and she flexed and stretched her fingers to get the blood circulating again.

"A chopper's coming," Officer Bowers said. "Do you think the Chief ordered one in?"

In minutes a large helicopter landed on

the shore and the slim figure of a young woman climbed out. The police officers kept their guns trained on their prisoners while watching the trim figure run toward them, the whole scene framed in the helicopter's landing lights.

The woman looked familiar but until she spoke, Linn did not recognize her. When she was about fifteen feet away, Officer Bowers ordered, "That's close enough, young lady. What's your business here?"

The girl stopped but called urgently, "I have a message for Mrs. Randolph from her husband!"

For a confused moment Linn could not take it in. This person dressed in designer jeans and field boots with a dark braid hanging down her back and no subtle make-up could not be Bonnie Leeds — but it was!

"Clay sent a message for you." Bonnie turned her dark velvet gaze on Linn. "He's been in a car accident. Your aunt is hurt and. . . ."

Linn did not wait for permission from the police officers. All she could think of was that Kate was hurt and maybe the others. She rushed to Bonnie.

"How badly is Aunt Kate hurt?" she asked anxiously. "Was anyone else hurt?"

"I have a note for you right here," Bonnie said. She stuck her hand inside the denim jacket she wore and came out with a small deadly pistol in her shapely hand. It was leveled squarely at Linn's chest!

Linn sucked in her breath and drew back but Bonnie took a step forward. The gun touched Linn's shirt.

"Don't move or I'll put a bullet right through your heart," Bonnie said in her soft, husky voice. Linn looked into Bonnie's black eyes, smoldering with hate, and knew she meant it.

"I have a gun aimed at Mrs. Randolph's heart," Bonnie called to the police officers. "And there is a rifle in the helicopter trained on you. Throw down your weapons and come over here. Lie face down on the ground."

Linn didn't dare move, so she couldn't see if the policemen were obeying.

"Move! That's right! That's close enough. Lie down — easy now."

Even with fear threatening to paralyze her, Linn was amazed at Bonnie's sergeant-like manner. Questions poured through her mind. Was Bonnie a smuggler now? If so, why? She was extremely wealthy. How had she gotten mixed up with Carlos?

Carlos and Bonnie! Of course! That was where she had seen Carlos before. In The Gull's Nest restaurant — with Bonnie. Horrible comprehension widened her eyes. Bonnie was Carlos's partner in an art treasure smuggling operation!

Bonnie's composed voice was giving more orders. "Frank, gather up those weapons. Carlos, how bad is Juan hurt? Can he travel? Good. Why don't you get Diego from the chopper and load that stuff into the helicopter. We've got to get out of here. I hear a boat coming and a chopper. Frank, search those two officers."

The search was completed swiftly and thoroughly, and Bonnie barked out more orders. "Now, handcuff that older policeman's hands behind his back. Get that other one up on his feet again."

Helplessly, Linn could only listen to the activity going on behind her back. She couldn't see anything and did not dare move. She could sense that Bonnie would relish any opportunity to use her gun on Linn.

"Okay, copper, you're going to call off your buddies! Get on that car radio and tell them we have hostages. If anyone comes close or if there is a plane or helicopter in sight when we take off, we won't be responsible for your health or the two ladies. Now get with it! Move!"

As Linn heard Bonnie bawling orders in a brutal tone and saw her swaggering stance, she could scarcely believe this was the wealthy socialite. Bonnie's acting was superlative.

And the disguise was perfect. This strutting, cold-voiced lady bandit would never be recognized in the delicately painted face and softly husky voice of the sophisticated Bonnie Leeds. It was incredible!

"Now, Miz Randolph, you get down in the sand on your face! Give me any trouble, and it'll be the last thing you ever do."

The intense malice in Bonnie's voice left Linn no choice. She obeyed.

Officer Guffrey had made his call on the police radio and now he and his partner were handcuffed back to back.

Carlos approached and whispered in Bonnie's ear. A short, evil laugh was Bonnie's only response.

Within minutes, the contraband was loaded into the helicopter, the two policemen were gagged and left handcuffed to the outside of their car. The tires were quickly ruined by bullets from a gun with a silencer.

"I think we should leave Josie behind to take her punishment," Bonnie said to Carlos as they prepared to leave.

"Yes," Carlos said silkily in his cultured, pleasantly accented voice. "Josie, I hate disloyalty! I would have taken you with us but since you didn't want to admit your part in our plans, you can appease the lions of justice for all of us."

Josie said nothing. Despondently, she allowed herself to be handcuffed to the car with the two policemen.

Linn was also handcuffed and forced into the helicopter, sitting on the floor toward the back. Her fear was intense, but it was overshadowed by the fact that Josie had deceived her. Linn would have trusted Josie with her life and now to discover that she was the enemy . . . ! The knowledge was like a cold, solid tumor in Linn's stomach.

The helicopter rose into the night sky and Linn wondered dully if she was going to be ill. The helicopter was fighting heavy winds and a new downpour as the rain lashed at them again. Its jerking motions, the unrelenting tension, and her extreme disillusionment in Josie was beginning to upset Linn's stomach. She prayed, trying to relax in God's promise, "Fear not, for I am with you," realizing even as she prayed, that the nausea was beginning to subside.

I'm still alive and God is still on my side, she thought. *Things could be a lot worse.*

Bonnie moved back to sit down near Linn. The friendly light was back in her dark eyes and her voice was soft again. "Well, *Mrs.* Randolph! I suppose you're wondering what this is all about."

Linn ignored the sham of friendliness and asked, "What are you going to do with me, Bonnie?"

Bonnie's eyes seemed to darken and Linn saw cold, naked hate in them. Linn had seen Bonnie's lightning fast mood changes before, but they were always startling. One minute she was one person, the next entirely different.

Linn's inner alarm must have shown on her face and Bonnie saw it. She laughed lightly. "Linn, darling, you're not afraid of me, are you?"

Fighting her fear, Linn tried to speak as lightly as Bonnie. "Why should I be afraid of you, Bonnie?"

Bonnie's sinister, vindictive voice came clearly through the clamor of the helicopter and the storm. "Why, Linn? My promise. Remember the promise I made you once? I said I'd make you sorry you were ever born if you stood in the way of my marrying Clay — and I meant just that."

Linn tried to interrupt, but Bonnie's voice continued relentlessly.

"Are you frightened, Linn? You should be! I'm a moon shell, Linn — beautiful but deadly!" Bonnie laughed then, high, shrill and chilling. Its brittle tinkle sounded clearly, harshly harmonious with the fury of the storm.

Linn wondered, with dread attacking the wall of defense the Scripture had raised in her heart, if Bonnie was demented. Or was she a dual personality? No. Linn knew better. Bonnie was always in control. Linn had never seen her otherwise. But she was a clever, sadistic actress — and dangerous!

"Are you scared, Linn? If you aren't, you should be!" Bonnie's eyes took on a sly look. "Remember that adorable green snake you found in your closet?"

"You put it there?" Linn asked with certainty as to the answer.

Bonnie smirked evilly. "I never forgot your phobia, and we needed to drive you away from Moonshell. Carlos thought a good scare might do the trick. It didn't, but it was amusing watching you scramble away from that boa. You even fell down and cracked your head!"

Linn tried to keep her voice calm, though anger was very near the surface. It was anger she couldn't afford to show because it was imperative to get all the information possible from Bonnie.

"How did you manage to get the snake out of Alfred's room and into my room?"

Bonnie eyed Linn balefully for a moment, then she laughed cruelly. "I suppose it won't hurt to tell you. I wouldn't want you to die of curiosity." She put an unpleasant emphasis on "curiosity." "I have other plans for you."

Linn felt her scalp prickle.

"A secret passageway winds all through Moonshell. Through it one can reach any part of the house without being seen. Carlos and his men used it today. There is a hidden door to it at the back of the house."

"And you put the moon shells and threatening note in my room, too?"

"That was Carlos's idea, too!" Sudden scorn twisted Bonnie's delicate lips. "I would never have just threatened you! Never! But Carlos didn't want anyone killed! So I gave in and tried to use scare tactics to drive you away. But only twice!"

In spite of herself, Linn could not control the tremor in her voice. "So you were the one who tried to kill me? Both times?"

With mercurial speed the little demons of hate glittered in Bonnie's eyes again. "Yes, I was! And you survived both times — but you won't be so lucky this time!"

Bonnie's taunting laughter encircled Linn in a suffocating embrace but she steeled herself against panic. She wanted to learn all she could.

"How did you ever get mixed up with a smuggler, Bonnie? With your wealth, it seems so strange."

Bonnie laughed with merriment. "Boredom! When you've seen and experienced all the usual pleasures, one is always looking for new thrills." Bonnie leaned over and placed a soft, bejeweled hand on Linn's arm. "And Carlos is very handsome and dashing, don't you think?"

"How did you meet him?"

"I spent some time in Mexico quite a while back as the house guest of friends. Carlos was there for a weekend. We got to talking and I discovered he was searching for a place on the Texas coast to hide some priceless artifacts. Since I have the heart of a pirate myself, I decided to help him."

Bonnie chortled with glee. "I had met Clyde Cameron several years before and had been a guest in his home. He told me once that there were secret stairways and passageways in Moonshell but I didn't know where they were. I suggested to Carlos that he find out and arrange to store his treasures there. He did just that and we became partners."

Bonnie chuckled in malicious delight. "Imagine my amazement when I discovered you were the family occupying Moonshell for the summer. We had thought Clyde Cameron would be away and the house would be empty."

She chortled again. "But I knew Lady Fortune was smiling on me when I heard it was you at Moonshell! I could carry out my vow to you and get rid of the unwanted guests at the same time. I knew Clay would leave if there was any threat to his precious wife! But even if you ran like scared rats, I had planned to kill you before you could get away!"

Linn trembled as Bonnie talked about murder as casually as she would have about attending a party.

"Carlos was squeamish about murder, but when he saw it was the only way to get rid of you, he gave in. But he refused to do it himself! Oh well, I rather think I have an assassin's nature anyway, don't you?"

Linn let her eyes drop from the maniacal

gleam in Bonnie's eyes. It was frightening. She changed the subject. "Who told Carlos where the secret passageways were? Josie?"

Bonnie tilted back her head and sneered, "Wouldn't you like to know?"

"So what are you going to do with me?" Linn asked.

"You asked that before." Bonnie sat with her head slightly to one side and studied Linn for a moment, a malevolent, calculating expression on her face.

Suddenly, Linn felt an inexplicable, tremendous sense of the presence of God as she remembered that the old Linn would have hated as vehemently and plotted revenge just as Bonnie was doing. *But I am no longer bound by those desires to hurt and destroy,* she thought with exultation bubbling up inside her.

"Bonnie, why do you let hate and jealousy ruin your life?" Linn asked softly. "I'm sure you remember how I almost let them wreck my marriage. But I have found a better way and so has Clay. Can't we be friends and let the old days be a closed chapter in our lives?"

Bonnie leaped to her feet, anger blazing in her hatred-filled eyes. For a moment Linn thought Bonnie was going to strike her. "You're real pious, aren't you! You want to be friends!" Bonnie's voice was filled with fury. "You can afford to be righteous! You got Clay and he belonged to me!" Fire seemed to almost leap from her eyes. "Not that I want your precious Clay anymore! Carlos de la Zorro is more man than Clay Randolph ever was or will ever be!"

"Don't you see how futile this really is?" Linn tried to reason with Bonnie. "You could do so much good with your money and talents, if you would turn them over to God and let Him give you a truly satisfying life."

"I like my life!" Bonnie spat the words out maliciously. "So don't go pushing your religion on me!"

As Linn realized Bonnie's venom, dread filled her. Bonnie was a dangerous enemy and she knew that her life was in God's hands now.

Bonnie stood up and stabbed a slim finger in Linn's face. Her words were a cobra's hiss. "And now let me tell you what I'm going to do with you! You loved Moonshell, so I'll let you die inside her! I'm going to shut you up in that tight, vault-like room where we stored our treasures."

She lowered her voice to a sinister

whisper. "No one will know where you are and you will die there alone, in the dark. Even if the hurricane doesn't destroy the house, the storm surges will be high enough to drown you like a caged rat!"

Bonnie turned, fighting the tormented movement of the helicopter, and made her way back to Carlos.

Linn felt like she was in a tight, airless box as she labored to breathe. The picture Bonnie had painted was too real. Anguished words welled up and were uttered softly through lips pale with terror. "Dear God, help me now. Don't let this happen. Please, hear my prayer."

No spectacular display occurred, but as Linn prayed, peace gradually stilled her panic. Even if she died in that black, lonely hole, she knew she would not be alone.

The helicopter landed roughly in the dark, gale-filled night on the Moonshell lawn. Linn was hustled quickly outside.

"The storm is getting worse. Please hurry, Miss Leeds," the pilot shouted urgently.

Bonnie nodded her acknowledgment and pulled Linn roughly after her. Frank led the way through the darkened mansion and down into the boathouse. It didn't take them long to remove Linn's handcuffs and lock her in the small secret room.

"Goodbye, Linn, darling. Remember me when the water begins to run in. As it rises higher and higher and then closes over your head, remember that Bonnie Leeds has kept her promise to you!" Bonnie's taunting laughter floated back as their footsteps faded away.

28

When the panel slipped into place shutting Linn into the total darkness of the small storeroom, new panic rose like bile into her throat.

"Easy, Linn," she said aloud. "Remember that God promised to be with you always and that means here, too. Besides, God knows you are here and I firmly believe He will get you out of here!" And suddenly, she did believe that!

Sitting down on an empty wooden box — the only item in the room — she propped her back against the wall. She might as well be as comfortable as possible.

She touched the cool, concrete floor of the storeroom. It felt a little gritty, but so far it was dry! She remembered someone saying that sometimes during a hurricane, a storm surge or tidal wave could rise high enough to engulf whole sections of coastal towns. She wondered how long it would take for the bay to rise.

She felt the floor again. Would she hear the water coming in or would it just rise slowly and silently into this small room? A prickle of terror shot through her.

"Cut it out, Linn!" she said sternly. "You can't dwell on this sort of thing."

With an effort she forced herself to think of the events of the past few hours. Bonnie had certainly cleared up much of the mystery surrounding this place. Bonnie's evil revenge had been at the root of everything. Linn shivered as she remembered the poisoned dates. *If I hadn't had morning sickness, I would have eaten some dates before poor little Baby did,* she thought. *But I still don't know for sure who told Carlos about this hidden storeroom and the secret passageways. Could Josie really be guilty?*

Linn's every instinct rebelled against such a thought, but Carlos had said she did. And he had certainly treated her differently when they were first captured. Josie had definitely known him.

But surely Josie had not accepted any money from him, or she wouldn't have been so worried about money to start college on. And I can hardly suspect Alfred of helping Carlos. He's only fifteen. Mrs. Benholt is grumpy, but a good sort really, as well as an excellent housekeeper.

Maybe the whole Benholt family is helping the smugglers, she thought. *They are always in desperate need of money to finance the twins' education. And they would need more money yet when Alfred entered college.*

But if Joe had known the smugglers were using this place, surely he wouldn't have told Clay about the shopping center being for sale. But he might not have anticipated Clyde Cameron inviting them to use his house. After all, if the shopping center sold, then Clyde would take his trip to Scotland and Moonshell should have been clear for the smugglers to use.

Linn shook her head as the futile speculations chased themselves round and round. Truthfully, it was hard to imagine any of the Benholts doing anything dishonest. They had their internal family problems, but they were hard working and seemed the epitome of honesty and dependability.

It was mind boggling. Linn knew that she didn't know enough yet to decide who, if anyone, at Moonshell was in alliance with the smugglers.

A muffled noise drew her attention. It was the sound of someone opening the doors to the boat garage!

Had the smugglers returned? Could it be the redheaded spy taking advantage of everyone's absence? If so, why?

Linn could hear the sound of a motorboat put-putting into the boathouse, and the low murmur of voices. Should she call? Doubt chased fear in her mind. She was frightened in this close, dark room, but was there safety beyond it?

Suddenly a bass, male voice called, "Mrs. Randolph, are you in here somewhere?"

Linn held her breath, her mind working frantically. It wasn't Carlos or Bonnie. Could it be the police? Her heart leaped in hope.

"Mrs. Randolph, this is the Coast Guard. If you are here somewhere, please come out."

Linn tried to call but only a weak sound came out. She tried again, this time loudly. "I'm here! Locked in a hidden storeroom!"

Almost instantly Linn heard the bump of a boat alongside the concrete dock, and scraping and crunching as men climbed from the boat. Then she heard the sound of at least two men's feet approaching the wall of her prison.

"How can we get into where you are?"

the same male voice asked.

"I'm not sure," Linn said, "but there may be a catch in a little notch in the baseboard."

She could hear the murmur of low voices as the men searched for the catch. Suddenly a different voice spoke. It sounded like the voice of the young policeman, Ted Guffrey. "Here!"

And almost instantly a small gleam of light broke into Linn's prison. She blinked and tried to adjust her eyes as the panel slipped noiselessly back into the wall and more light flooded the room.

"Wow! That's terrific!" exclaimed Officer Guffrey — for it was, indeed, the young policeman.

The other man was the redheaded fisherman-spy. His hairy face crinkled into a smile, "My name is Bob Jarvis and I'm Coast Guard. Ted, here, got me on my radio and said the smugglers' helicopter was heading this way. So I hid and watched them bring you inside Moonshell and leave without you. I had to wait until I was sure they were gone before I came looking for you. By that time Ted had arrived."

"Am I ever glad to see you!" Linn could have hugged the rough-looking Coast Guardsman. She was so glad to be free!

"But how did you get here?" Linn asked.

"A police chopper came in as soon as the smugglers' chopper was out of sight. We called Bob, who was still in the vicinity, and then we came right on over in the police helicopter."

"I suppose you've been watching Moonshell because of the smugglers?" Linn asked Bob. "I saw you, but didn't know why you were spying on Moonshell."

"We've suspected for some time that extremely valuable Mexican artifacts were being hidden at Moonshell. But we didn't know by whom or where."

"We still don't know for sure who, at Moonshell, has been working with the smugglers," Ted Guffrey said. "As you know, Mrs. Randolph, Carlos de la Zorro implicated Miss Benholt. Do you think she is guilty?"

Linn hesitated. "I can hardly believe she would do such a thing, but I honestly do not know."

"Money can make nice people do some bad things," Bob Jarvis said grimly.

"Where is Josie — Miss Benholt?" Linn asked.

"She's out in the helicopter. We're transporting her — and you as a witness — to the San Antonio area, away from the storm," Ted said. "And we had better be on our way before this storm gets any worse."

The wind tore at their clothes and whipped the heavy rain, bits of grass, twigs and sand about them as they sprinted to the helicopter. As Linn ran, she wondered how safe a helicopter was in this kind of wind.

She also rather dreaded seeing Josie. But in a moment she was seated beside her in the helicopter. Linn spoke to her and Josie mumbled a return greeting.

As soon as they were in the air, Josie turned to Linn. Her face registered hurt and unbelief. "Linn, you think I'm part of the smuggling ring!" she accused.

Linn lifted bewildered eyes to Josie. "I don't know what I think!" she said. "You must admit everything looks suspicious. And Carlos declares you are."

"He would!" Josie said angrily. "He feels I've rejected him and so he's doing this to spite me."

"So you are his girlfriend?"

"Never!" Josie said vehemently. "Two years ago, Carlos was a house guest at Moonshell. He kept flirting with me and I'll admit I was very flattered at his attentions. He kept trying to get me alone and one day I consented to go for a walk with him. Then he asked for a real date and I accepted."

Josie paused as if remembering. "When Joe heard about it he was furious. The gossip was that Carlos might be engaged in shady business of some sort and Joe had heard it. Joe and Mother raised such a rumpus that I called Carlos and broke the date."

Josie clutched Linn's arm with tense, cold fingers. "I swear I have never even seen or heard from Carlos again until today."

"Why did he keep you out on the deck with him?"

"At first he said he needed me out there to do the talking if we were stopped. He said he would tie you and me both up and dump us in the Gulf if I didn't do what he asked. I was afraid not to."

"Then?"

"Then, after we had gotten past that bearded man in the green and silver boat, he called me over close to him and began to sweet talk me. He said he had never forgotten me and wanted me for his sweetheart. He promised to dress me with beautiful clothes and jewels and treat me like a queen."

Josie's eyes filled with tears and she

dropped her eyes. "That man frightens me. Even when I was attracted to Carlos, he frightened me. Maybe that was part of the fascination as sheltered and naive as I was."

Brushing the tears away, Josie looked right in Linn's eyes. "You may think I'm a coward, and I suppose I am, but at first when Carlos began to say all of those sweet things, I didn't say much of anything. I was terrified of him so I did lots of praying and tried not to think of what Carlos might do to us if we angered him.

"That worked for awhile and then Carlos began to press me to express my feelings for him. When I tried to be evasive, he finally became angry and grabbed me by the shoulders and shook me. So then I flatly told him that I wanted nothing to do with him."

"And that's why he told the policeman you were a part of the ring?"

"Right! Let me tell you, I was thrilled to see those policemen! Carlos would have carried out his threat and dumped us in the Gulf! He was furious with me!"

"He would be capable, I'm sure," Linn agreed. "And I do believe your story, Josie. What really set me to wondering about you was when I saw that you knew Carlos and he treated you differently than he did me.

Then I recalled how you were supposed to stay in the car but you came right up to my room when I went to look for my purse."

"I came up to your room," Josie explained, "because as soon as you were gone, I recalled seeing your purse on the car seat earlier. I wondered if someone was up to something.

"But believe me, Linn. I was as surprised to see Carlos and his accomplices as you were!"

"I believe you," Linn said. "And I am so sorry I doubted you. Everything's getting to me, I guess."

"Under the same circumstances, I likely would have doubted you, too," Josie said forgivingly. "Let's just forget it."

"But now we're back to the same old question," Linn said. "Who sold Carlos an entrance into Moonshell?"

"I wish I knew," Josie said.

"Josie," Linn said after a few moments of silence, "do you think Joe was allowing those men to use Moonshell to store their contraband — for a price?"

Josie sighed. "I've been turning that horrible possibility over in my mind. Joe told me a while back he is working on securing a grant that would put us both through our remaining years of medical school. But he said if I didn't go along with him about everything, I wouldn't get any of it. So it could be money, rather than a grant, that he is getting. I can't imagine what has gotten into him, anyway."

"Of course we don't know for sure that he's the one who let those smugglers use Moonshell," Linn said. "Just a short while ago I was suspecting you," she finished ruefully.

"No, but who else could have? And how else could he obtain the kind of money he was talking about?"

Linn agreed it did sound suspicious.

They sat for a few minutes, each wrapped in her own thoughts. Suddenly Josie spoke. "Linn, could I talk to you about something?" She paused, color staining her cheeks pink.

"I-I-I'm in love — with Eric." Josie stopped as if searching for the right words, then blurted out a question. "I thought he cared, too. So what happened? Did I say or do something to drive him away?"

Linn considered carefully before she answered, realizing that her words would carry much weight with Josie. "I thought he liked you very much, too," she said slowly. "But Eric has been a confirmed bachelor for a long time. I don't know why he turned so suddenly to a wild crowd. But it wasn't you! I think Eric Ford may just be afraid of marriage and is running from his feelings."

"Maybe that's it," Josie said sadly. "I tried hard not to fall for him but it just happened. I didn't seem to have any control over it at all."

"I know what you mean," Linn sympathized. "Love is a sneaky thing. But God's in control of even our feelings."

"I know," Josie agreed. "I'm trusting Him hard for that."

A change in the pitch of the helicopter engine signaled their approach to landing.

"Linn, do you think I'll be put in jail?" Josie asked fearfully.

"I don't know, but I'll do everything in my power to keep that from happening," Linn promised.

29

Differences forgotten, Clay and Eric began their drive back to Moonshell. They were not far on their journey when the rain began to fall. Soon it was coming down so hard it was difficult for the wipers to keep the windshield clear enough to drive.

Although the traffic going toward the coast was light, the heavy rain slowed them down. About dawn they drove up the gravel drive to Moonshell. The first thing they saw was Linn's car parked in the drive.

The wind which had been buffeting the car with increasing force the closer they came to the coast, almost tore the car doors from their hands when they tried to get out. Forcing the doors shut, the two fought their way to Linn's car, yanked open a door and peered inside. They saw only the suitcases in the otherwise empty car. Clay slammed the door. With heads bent against the wind and half-blinded by the sheets of rain, they toiled their way toward the porch.

They had gone just a few steps when they heard a shout from the porch. Above the howl of the wind and the pounding rain, it sounded like, "Run!" Then it came again. Louder and more urgent this time. "Run! This way!"

Clay was ahead of Eric and he put all his strength into his effort to fling himself toward the voice. Ducking his head lower against the lashing elements, he plunged forward and was almost to the porch when he heard a terrible rending and ripping sound followed only seconds later by a deafening crash.

Another leap and he gained the porch. Turning around, through the driving rain he made out the outline of a monstrous tree lying on the ground. A huge, live-oak tree, perhaps centuries old, had fallen victim to the fury of the storm.

Suddenly the bloodthirsty leech of horror latched itself on Clay. Eric wasn't with him on the porch! Clay searched the ground he had so recently crossed with fearful eyes. The giant tree filled that ground. Eric must be under the tree!

His shock and fear were so great that he

was hardly aware of the man who stood behind him until he spoke.

"Come on," the man shouted, "the tree fell on him!" And springing from the porch the man began plowing through the storm toward the fallen tree. It was the red-headed, bearded fisherman!

"Dear God, don't let Eric die without being prepared to stand before You," Clay cried out as he followed on the run. Panic and fear clawed at him, but he pushed them away. He couldn't afford the doubtful luxury of feeling anything right now.

The other man was already pawing through the massive, outspread branches, searching for Eric. Clay stood for a second, the blinding torrents pouring down upon him, trying to think where Eric would most likely be under the heavy foliage. Considering their path from the car, he was sure the other man was a little too far north.

Selecting the spot he thought should be about right, he waded into the sea of leaves, twigs and branches. Feeling carefully with feet and hands, Clay moved cautiously forward.

Suddenly he thought he heard a moan just at his feet. Falling on his knees, he felt around in the springy branches and leaves and found a hand. "He's over here!" Clay yelled to the other man as he fought to push through the thick foliage.

The big fisherman joined Clay and together they carefully extricated Eric from the clinging arms of the huge fallen tree. As they pulled him from beneath a heavy branch, Eric struggled to sit up. Raising his arms to fit around their necks, they half-carried, half-dragged him up onto the porch. Laying him down, Clay found his house key and opened the door.

Eric sat up, shaking his head groggily. When Clay knelt beside him, he asked shakily, "Did the sky fall on me?"

Relief bubbled up inside Clay. Eric didn't seem too badly hurt. "You had a race with a live-oak tree and it won," he said, grinning. "Now, let us help you into the house."

When they had Eric stretched out on an enormous couch in the living room, the red-haired man insisted on checking Eric over. A large goose egg on Eric's forehead was already swelling angrily, and one leg was badly bruised below the knee.

"I would say you are a very lucky man," the stranger declared. "When I saw you go down under that tree, I wouldn't have given two cents for your life!"

"I believe God would call it more than luck!" Clay said emphatically.

Eric cast a quick glance at Clay and then away. "I think maybe you're right," he said solemnly.

The tall fisherman looked from one to the other and cleared his throat self-consciously.

Clay stood up. "I've got to go see if I can find the girls." He was half-way out of the room when the fisherman yelled, "Hey, I know where your wife is!"

Clay stopped dead and spun around. "You do? Where?" he demanded anxiously.

"She's in Poteet, a little city just this side of San Antonio."

Clay walked back across the room, a puzzled expression on his face. "In Poteet? What's she doing there? Is she safe?"

Eric broke in. "Is Josie there, too? There were two girls."

"They're both fine," the man said.

"What are they doing there?" Clay reiterated.

Instead of answering, the redheaded fisherman asked a question of his own, "Mr. Randolph, do you know who I am?"

"Only that you have been watching our house from a boat in the bay."

"I'm Bob Jarvis, a Coast Guardsman.

Moonshell has been suspected of being the hiding place for stolen Mexican artifacts for some time. We've had it under surveillance for weeks."

"I don't know anything about any artifacts being hidden at Moonshell," Clay said. "And besides, what has that to do with my wife?" he asked impatiently.

"A lot!" Bob Jarvis declared. "Yesterday your wife walked in on the smugglers moving their contraband from a storage place at Moonshell and they kidnapped her."

Clay grabbed Bob's arm in a tense grip, "Has someone harmed Linn?"

"Easy, Mr. Randolph," Bob cautioned. "I told you she's all right and she is. The smugglers are in custody but we needed your wife along for her testimony against the thieves."

"And Josie? She's okay, too?" Eric asked.

The guardsman looked doubtful. "I'm not sure of all that's going on, but I think she is being held as part of the smuggling ring."

Eric was aghast. "That's impossible! Didn't Linn tell you that she could never be a part of something like that?"

"Say, fellows, I don't know a whole lot about it all. Why don't you wait and find out for yourselves. Right now we've got to get out of here while we can."

"Why are you still here?" asked Clay as they walked to the door.

"Mrs. Randolph asked if I would wait for you. She knew you'd come back for her and be frantic. I was about to give up, though."

Pausing with his hand on the doorknob, he stroked his beard thoughtfully. "Let me tell you briefly what happened. You see, we were expecting the smugglers to move their contraband because of the hurricane warnings. So we had a twenty-four hour surveillance set up. We never saw them come in, at least not by water. I don't know yet how they got into Moonshell without our seeing them.

"I was out in my boat yesterday afternoon, watching the house, when the Moonshell yacht came out of the boathouse! Miss Benholt and a man were on deck. The man kept pretty well turned away from me but I think he was a stranger. Miss Benholt did the talking and said they were taking the yacht to safer waters in Copano Bay.

"We alerted the Coast Guard and police up and down the coast to stand by, so the yacht was immediately spotted when it docked in Copano Bay. All the policemen had to do was go in and pick them up. But some girl pulled a fast one and the smugglers got away."

Clay whistled. "This must have been a big operation to put so much time and so many men on it!"

"It is. Those artifacts are almost invaluable to Mexico. They're very old and some of the best pieces found to date. They would probably sell for millions on the market.

"Carlos de la Zorro, a wealthy Mexican playboy, has been the chief suspect for a long time but we have never been able to catch him with any of the goods. They were probably brought in a few at a time in a small fishing boat. So we knew he had to be hiding them somewhere on the U.S. side of the Gulf."

"Why did you suspect they were being hidden at Moonshell?" Clay asked.

"We saw a small motorboat coming out of the Moonshell canal a couple of times but they got away from us. We soon learned that Moonshell had no such boat. Also, the stolen artifacts' trail was always lost in this vicinity."

"I still say Josie had nothing to do with that smuggling ring," Eric spoke up angrily, his previous disregard forgotten.

Bob held up his hand as a gesture of peace. "And I don't know. But we'd better get on the road before it becomes impossible."

30

The drive to Poteet was wild and nerve-racking. Driving rain and gusty winds pounded and rocked their cars. It took constant vigilance to stay on the highway. Bob Jarvis led the way in his car with Clay and Eric following. Thankfully the road was almost void of motor vehicles.

Eric volunteered to help drive but Clay wouldn't allow it. He could see that Eric was in pain from his severely bruised left leg, and the huge bump on his forehead. Clay was insistent that as soon as they arrived at their destination, he was taking Eric to a doctor.

Throughout the drive the news on the car radio painted a grim picture. Small tornadoes, spawned by the hurricane, were touching down here and there. The entire area from the Gulf of Mexico to beyond San Antonio was in the danger area. It didn't take a vivid imagination to picture a tornado materializing out of the chaos they were traveling through. Clay's nerves were taut.

Eric didn't talk much on the trip. It was almost impossible anyway above the sound of the raging wind and rain. But once, when he had been quiet for a long while with his eyes closed, and Clay thought he was asleep, Eric abruptly broke the silence, speaking almost as if to himself.

"I could have died back there under that tree! I didn't even know it was falling till it floored me. One minute I was running through the rain and the next minute I was on the ground. It felt like I was wrapped in a thousand octopus tentacles and they were smothering me to death. The huge limb that caused the knot on my head was lying right next to me. It was so close, I couldn't even move my arm. The branch that pinned me was its lighter cousin."

Clay saw him shudder as he relived the horrendous ordeal. "I just thank God you are still alive," Clay said. "But why don't you try to forget about it and go back to sleep."

"I haven't been asleep," Eric said. "I've been thinking about how near I came to death and that I wasn't ready to stand before God." Another tremor passed through his body.

"You can remedy that any time you want," Clay said. "God will accept you right now if you want Him to."

Eric was silent. Clay felt that he had again drawn back. Why? Why could Eric not make that simple little step and settle his future? But all Clay could do for his friend was silently petition God to somehow make Eric realize that it was dangerous to put off receiving Christ. How much closer to death would he have to come?

When they pulled into Poteet, it was mid-morning and still pouring rain like it planned to go on forever.

Bob inquired at the jail for Josie's and Linn's whereabouts. He was informed that due to lack of jail space, with so many prisoners being brought in from the coast, Josie had been allowed to stay in a motel room with Linn.

A few minutes later Clay had Linn in his arms and was assured she was unharmed.

Eric embraced Josie with such warmth that it brought the stars back to Josie's expressive dark eyes.

Clay put in a call to Clawson Campground and learned that the wind had blown down one tent and the increasingly heavy rain and tornado danger had forced everyone into the campground's recreation room. Joe relayed that it was crowded, but certainly better than being out in the storm in a tent.

When he learned that Josie was a suspect in Carlos de la Zorro's smuggling ring, he went into a rage, declaring that he should have known Josie wouldn't stay away from the hoodlum.

Exasperated that Joe was so quick to assume Josie's guilt, Clay cut him off sharply. "Joe, your sister swears she had nothing to do with the smuggling or with Carlos. Linn, Eric and I believe her. And she could use some support from her family right now!"

Joe was silent for a minute and then he said grudgingly, "Perhaps I am being a little hasty in my judgment. We'll be there as soon as we can. I'll see if Mrs. Marshall and Penny will watch our belongings while we're gone." And he hung up.

But a few hours later when he, Mrs. Benholt and Alfred entered the motel room where Josie, Linn, Clay and Police Officer Guffrey were assembled, Joe immediately began to condemn Josie unmercifully.

Josie's face paled as she tried to explain but Joe refused to listen. His face distorted with anger, he yelled, "I've always sus-pected you were carrying on behind our backs with that sneaky —"

Eric jumped to his feet and interrupted. "That will be enough! You can't talk to Josie like that!"

Joe turned his blazing eyes on Eric. "I'll talk to her any way I please. She's my sister! And you keep out of this!"

Officer Guffrey stood up, alert and ready.

Clay put a restraining hand on Eric's shoulder, but spoke to Joe. "Why don't you calm down and at least let Josie give you her explanation."

But Joe refused to be placated. "I don't need an explanation. It's as obvious as the storm out there that she's guilty! And to think that my sister would stoop to this! Not only sneaking out to be with that — that brigand, but letting those hoodlums right into our house! They could have murdered us all in our beds!"

"Lay off of Josie!"

Everyone looked around, startled. It was Alfred. He was so angry that his face was ashy-white; the freckles sprinkled across his nose and cheekbones stood out like dark brown beads.

"Josie didn't make the deal with Carlos,"

Alfred said belligerently. "I did! So shut your mouth, Joe."

Mrs. Benholt gasped and then began to sputter, "Of course you didn't, Alfred! You're just trying to protect your sister!"

Alfred was trembling but adamant. "I did do it! And Joe has no right to pick on Josie like that! He's not her boss!"

Josie's eyes filled with tears. "Alfred, I appreciate what you're trying to do, but we all know you had nothing to do with the smugglers. Don't worry, I'm not guilty and the court will set me free."

Alfred looked around the circle of stunned faces with an amazed expression on his face. Then he sighed deeply, "Can't I get it through everyone's head that I'm the one who gave Carlos a key to the boathouse? And I'm the one who went down and took down the safety bar on the door every time Carlos called and told me a shipment was coming in. I did it!"

"I don't believe it!" Joe ejaculated.

"I can prove it!" Alfred declared.

"Ha! This I've got to see!" Joe said scornfully.

Officer Guffrey had stood quietly by, but now he took command. "I would like to hear this young man's story and see his proof."

There was bedlam then as Alfred's family all began talking at once, denying that Alfred could possibly have had any part in the smuggling and protesting to his being interrogated.

"He will be questioned anyway, so it might be best if I hear his story right now. If I place no credence in it, he will most likely not be called in for questioning at all," the policeman said.

Reluctantly, the Benholts agreed to let Alfred tell his story.

"I first saw Carlos de la Zorro a couple of years ago when he was a guest at Moonshell," Alfred began, "but I never talked to him or anything. Then about six months ago I met Carlos on the beach a little way from the house. I had heard the stories that he might be a smuggler and I guess I thought of him as a kind of storybook, modern day pirate. I was thrilled when he struck up a conversation with me."

Joe snorted disdainfully at this, but Alfred just threw him a dirty look and continued. "Carlos mentioned that he had a high-powered racing boat and asked if I would like a ride. Of course I did, so he took me out for a nice spin. After that, off and on for a couple of weeks Carlos had me clean and shine up his boat and do

300

some other chores for him. He paid me more than anyone ever had before.

"Then," Alfred said, "one day Carlos asked if I'd like to make some big money. I said sure. By this time," Alfred admitted, "I felt obligated. And besides, I was captivated by the air of charm about him. I felt honored to be called his friend.

"Carlos told me he had purchased some goods and needed a safe place to store them for a few months. He didn't tell me what the goods were, but he impressed upon me that I could tell no one that they were hidden at Moonshell."

Alfred looked ashamed. "I suspected I might be helping hide stolen or smuggled merchandise, but by that time I was beginning to be afraid of Carlos. His eyes are scary when he's even a little displeased."

And the thought of that big money had been extremely alluring. Carlos had promised to pay Alfred a hundred dollars each time a cache was delivered and a hundred dollars a month while the wares were stored at Moonshell.

"Carlos kept his word. I now have a thousand dollars in a savings account." His mother gasped in shock at this bit of information. "And if you don't believe it, I'll show you!"

He drew from his pocket a small packet, wrapped in plastic. Inside was a little bank record book. He handed it to the policeman. "There's the proof I'm telling the truth!"

Everyone crowded around to see. There were ten deposits of one hundred dollars each, with a total balance of $1,000.00 in a savings account which bore the name of Alfred L. Benholt. Alfred was telling the truth!

Shocked silence reigned in the room. Finally Linn asked, "How did you know about the secret storeroom in the boat garage?"

"Clyde Cameron, Moonshell's owner, was a little drunk one time and he showed it to me, and the secret passageways, too," Alfred said. "He said he believed the storeroom had been used by the original builders to store their valuables when they were away from home."

"Did the iguana pendant that you gave Penny come from Carlos's stolen artifacts?" asked Clay.

Alfred hung his head in remorse. "I really did find the necklace, but not on the beach. It was lying on the dock in the boathouse one night after Carlos had been there. It was so pretty and I knew Penny would love it, so I gave it to her. I hoped Carlos wouldn't miss it."

"But he did," Linn said.

"Yes. He met me on the beach the next morning and told me the pendant was a special prize. He had been taking it home with him and it must have slipped out of his pocket. At first I denied finding it but I guess I'm not a very good liar. He grabbed me and shook me till I almost lost my breath and told me to get the necklace or else. That's why I had to steal it back the next morning."

"He still had it," Linn said. "Josie and I saw it with the other stolen artifacts before they were packed."

31

Linn ambled slowly along the beach north of Moonshell, stopping occasionally to pick up a shell or a bit of driftwood. Her mind was not really on shell collecting, though. It was full of the events of the past two weeks — since the day they had fled the hurricane.

Fortunately the hurricane had weakened before it hit the Texas coast, and had moved inland at Brownsville, many miles south of the Rockport/Corpus Christi area. Storm surges had climbed nineteen to twenty-three feet above average in the Brownsville area Damage had been counted into the millions.

The damage at Rockport had been minimal. High winds had torn down trees; a few homes in low lying areas had flooded, and some docks and beaches were damaged. However, nowhere had the hurricane been as destructive as feared.

It's still a shock to realize that Alfred was

guilty of giving Carlos entry into Moonshell, Linn mused. *I would have suspected anyone else before Alfred. That goes to show one should never jump to conclusions.*

The judge had released Alfred into his mother's custody and it seemed unlikely that he would be punished any further because of his youth and because he had never been in any kind of trouble before. The experience seemed to have thoroughly chastened Alfred. He did not even lash back at Joe when he gave him a stern lecture.

Alfred had said he had never thought others might be in danger when he'd agreed to help Carlos. He was deeply sorry that Linn and Josie had suffered for his mistake.

Linn smiled as she remembered how Alfred had come to Penny afterward and contritely begged her forgiveness for stealing the necklace from her room. Penny had promptly accepted his apologies and they were as close as ever.

With the danger removed, they had decided to stay the remainder of the summer and everyone was enjoying Moonshell again. In fact, since Eric's close brush with death under the monstrous, old live-oak tree, Eric had been working faithfully. He hadn't said anything more about committing his life to God, yet, but Linn and Clay were hopeful that it wouldn't be long.

The only unresolved problem was his attitude toward Josie. Since she had been cleared of all wrongdoing, Eric hadn't spoken to her or of her to anyone.

Linn glanced at her watch. It was almost one o'clock; she must be getting back to the house. Clay would soon be home and they planned to join a party of workers at the church this afternoon helping to remodel the Sunday School annex. Then tonight she and Clay, Kate, Penny, Eric and Josie were invited to a dinner party at Esteban Molinas's home again.

As she started back toward the house, Linn gratefully recalled Bob Jarvis's recent phone call to Clay. He had told them that Carlos and his accomplices — including Bonnie — had been captured in Mexico when the extreme weather forced down their helicopter before they reached their hideaway. The fortune in art treasures had been recovered with the smugglers. They would stand trial in Mexico where each would probably receive a long sentence.

Bob had also told Linn that the woman who had taken pictures of Moonshell was an undercover agent. In fact, she wasn't a woman at all, but a policeman wearing a wig.

"We would never have found the artifacts by a search of Moonshell, though," Bob had said. "So the hurricane did us a favor. It scared the crooks right out into the open, treasures and all."

As Linn crossed the little canal footbridge, she saw Clay's car entering the drive and hastened her steps. She felt vibrantly alive and healthy today. She had had a check-up two weeks ago and again yesterday. Dr. Powell had confirmed that she was in excellent shape, and the baby's heartbeat strong. The rough treatment had not harmed either one.

Linn waited for Clay by the front door. She was surprised when he brushed her cheek lightly and went absentmindedly into the house.

Puzzled, Linn followed Clay up to their bedroom where she found him out on the balcony, staring out at the Gulf. Dread certainty gripped her.

"Eric's not coming to the dinner party tonight, is he?" she asked softly from behind Clay's back.

Slowly he turned. Linn could see the anguish in his eyes. "That girl — her name's Sylvia — picked him up in her red convertible about noon today. I haven't seen him since."

A black, shadowy depression settled over Linn. "Oh, Clay! It's as if he were caught in the web of a black widow spider and there's no escape for him."

"I know," Clay said, folding Linn tightly into his arms.

"Eric's been a part of the family so long. . . . It's like losing my best friend and favorite big brother all at once." Linn's voice broke as she realized how far beyond their reach Eric had slipped once again.

In the two weeks left before they had to leave Moonshell, Josie never mentioned Eric. If he was still in her thoughts and heart, she didn't say. Linn could tell that she was joyfully anticipating the return to her studies at medical school. She seldom went anywhere but to church and the library — from which she returned with large, heavy volumes on human anatomy and related subjects, devouring them voraciously.

Ellen Haskins was able to persuade Josie to attend a church party and a nice young man, Paul Curtis, brought her home afterward. The next day, though, Josie confided to Linn that Paul had asked her out, but she just wasn't interested in dating, so she had declined. Linn guessed that Eric was the main reason Josie was not interested in dating, but had discreetly said nothing.

Clay and Linn were moving into an apartment in Corpus Christi for a few weeks while the shopping center was completed. Kate and Penny were returning home to Grey Oaks so Penny could be enrolled in her own school. Joe and Josie would be leaving for school before long and Moonshell would be closed up until the Camerons returned from their trip. Mrs. Benholt would be staying to take care of things as she always had.

"I've decided to train someone else to take care of things here," Clay confided regretfully to Linn just a few days before they were to move into town. "Hopefully we can get Eric to go back with us to Idaho. Maybe he'll get back on the right track there. I'm afraid he's even drinking now and that's something he has always steered clear of, even when it flowed freely at parties he attended."

The sorrow in Linn's heart over Eric mingled with the tinge of sorrow she felt at leaving the lovely, elegant Moonshell as they prepared to go their separate ways. She knew she would miss Josie and Alfred — and even the dictatorial, hair-trigger tempered Joe and their somewhat aloof mother.

But she was getting homesick for the woods, the clear running waters of Idaho and Grey Oaks, so she hoped it wouldn't be long until the shopping center was completed and a manager trained so she and Clay could go home.

On their last Sunday at Moonshell, the family attended church as usual. The pastor had invited them for Sunday dinner as a little farewell party. They returned home in the afternoon for a rest, and then went back for the evening service.

Linn was disappointed when she discovered that Pastor Haskins was not speaking on their last Sunday night. The visiting minister, a young seminary student, gave a faltering, simple message.

When the young minister began an impassioned plea for those who did not know God to come forward for prayer, Linn felt somewhat annoyed. Surely no one would respond. Then she felt guilty for feeling that way. The young man had delivered the message God had given him and done the best he could.

Suddenly Linn heard Josie, who was sitting beside her, draw in her breath sharply. Linn turned toward Josie in surprise and saw that the girl's face had blanched. Her lips formed a single word — "Eric."

Linn's eyes followed Josie's thunderstruck gaze. She was right! Standing before the young minister was Eric! The student-minister whispered a few words to Eric and knelt with him at the altar.

Clay's fingers reached out and grasped Linn's hand in a hard grip. "That's Eric!" he whispered in a stunned voice.

Linn nodded and they watched as Pastor Haskins joined the other minister and Eric. They were both talking to Eric while the song leader continued to lead the congregation in the invitation.

Linn's heart felt like it would beat out of her chest. They had prayed so long for Eric!

When the congregation was dismissed, Linn and Clay made their way as quickly as possible to the front of the church where the young minister was speaking with Eric.

As soon as Eric saw his friends, his face lit up and he smiled his old jaunty grin. "This old prodigal decided it was time to come home," he said simply.

The visiting minister moved away as Clay and Linn emotionally hugged their friend. Clay asked Eric in a husky voice, "What happened?"

Eric's face sobered and he spoke with utter sincerity. "It's strange, but not more than an hour ago I was at one of those wild parties I thought I liked so well. All of a sudden something deep inside me — almost like an audible voice — seemed to say, 'What are you doing here? You don't belong here!'

"And right there in the middle of the loud music and dancing and drunken laughter, I knew what I have been afraid to admit to myself. All my life I have been running away from anything that required an absolute commitment of me."

He paused and looked away. Then his eyes swung back and locked with Clay's. "I've been a coward. I was afraid I couldn't make the grade as a Christian — and the thought of marriage scared the liver out of me. So many end in divorce or worse yet, become a battleground."

"Those are natural feelings," Clay said gently. "Most of us are afraid of stepping out of our well-worn grooves and the older a person gets, the more frightening it becomes."

"But most of you didn't run away like I have been doing — and from the two things I desired more than anything — God and Josie. I really love Josie and was about to ask her to marry me. And I wanted ours to be a Christian home."

Eric frowned as if in pain. "Then this Sylvia gal called and said she wanted to see me. I was flattered. I had met her at one of Bonnie's parties and I was fascinated with her so I agreed to meet her. We went to one of those wild, exhilarating parties and I convinced myself that I wasn't ready — yet — to give up my freedom to God or a girl.

"And I have been the most miserable man in the world, trying to have fun! I realized a while ago that I detested the life I was living and I would rather shoot myself and get out of my misery than keep on like that! I remembered there was church tonight, so here I am!"

"Where's Sylvia?" asked Clay.

"She ridiculed me for wanting to leave the party when it was just getting under way. When I left she was dancing with one man and batting her big blue eyes at another," Eric said ruefully.

"Would you like to go home with us?" asked Linn.

For a moment Eric's eyes searched the crowd and when he spoke, he responded to her question with another. "How's Josie? Is she all right?"

"Why don't you ask her yourself?" Clay said. "She's here somewhere."

Eric's face looked grim. "I've treated her abominably. Do you think she'll even let me talk to her?" His lips twisted in self-disgust, "Of all the fools in the world, I head the list!"

"She's probably in the car," Linn said. "Shall I ask her if she'll come back in?"

"Thanks, but I'll go. I could use a little moral support though."

When they arrived at Clay's station wagon a few minutes later, Josie was sitting in the back seat.

Clay and Linn hung back when Eric walked to the car and opened the door. "Hi, Josie," Eric said. "Can I speak with you?"

For a moment there was no answer and then they heard Josie's voice, polite and cool as an Idaho stream in the dead of winter. "If you like."

Eric reached in his hand and helped Josie from the car. His voice was low and humble. "Would you go over to the Sands Cafe with me — to talk. I'll bring you home."

For a long moment, Linn thought Josie was going to refuse. In the light from the church floodlights she could see Josie clearly. She looked every inch a regal little princess. Her soft curls shimmered and the dark eyes searching Eric's face were calm.

"Please," Eric said softly.

"Very well," Josie agreed distantly.

Eric took her arm, said good night to Clay and Linn, which was echoed by Josie, and they moved away down the line of parked vehicles to Eric's grey sedan.

"What do you think of that!" Clay marveled.

"It's great, but you're going to have to take me out for something to eat, too," Linn said archly. "I'm too excited to sleep for hours. I don't think I was any more excited when you asked me to marry you."

"If I remember correctly, you nearly bankrupted me that night, too," Clay groaned in mock dismay.

"I have an excuse now, dear husband," Linn giggled tenderly, holding his hand. "I'm eating for two."

32

The next morning Linn went down to breakfast with Clay. She was still excited about last night's events and anxious to see Josie.

But Josie didn't come to serve them, Mrs. Benholt did. The frown on her face accompanied her verbal complaints that Josie must still be sleeping as soon as they entered the room. "That's what comes of staying up all hours of the night going to church," she muttered crossly.

Clay and Linn exchanged glances. "I'll go and wake her," Linn volunteered.

"That's all right, I can manage," Mrs. Benholt said grudgingly, just as Kate and Penny appeared.

"I insist," Linn said and she hurried away upstairs. It wasn't like Josie to sleep in no matter how late she was out. Linn wanted to be sure she was all right.

A knock on Josie's door brought no response, so Linn turned the knob, opened the door a crack and called Josie's name softly. There was still no answer so Linn pushed the door open and entered. Josie was not in the room and the bed was neatly made.

Had Josie not come home last night? Or had she simply gotten up early and gone out somewhere? Neither was like Josie but she wasn't here!

When Linn came back downstairs and told Mrs. Benholt that Josie wasn't in her room, Mrs. Benholt asked quickly, "She came back home with you last night, didn't she?"

"Well, no," Linn admitted. "She went out with Eric after church."

"Eric Ford?" Mrs. Benholt's mouth tightened. "After that man dumped her, she still went out with him?" Receiving no answer, she went on, "She did come home last night, didn't she?"

When Linn said she didn't know, Mrs. Benholt whirled around and left the room. In less than a minute, Joe was in the room, the short leash on his temper obviously broken.

"What has that playboy done with my sister?" he demanded.

"Take it easy, Joe," Clay said. "I'm sure

Eric hasn't harmed Josie but it might be wise to see if perhaps there has been an accident. After I call my office, we'll make some calls to the hospitals and the police station."

Kate went on to the office, while Clay remained to help locate Josie. Clay called all the hospitals in the area and the police stations in both Rockport and Corpus Christi. No one had seen them. Linn and Clay's alarm was growing. Clay called the office again, hoping Eric had appeared for work. But Clay's secretary said Eric had not yet come in, and it was now ten-thirty.

"I'm going out to look for her!" Joe fumed. "And when I get my hands on that man I'm going to —"

Suddenly he stopped spewing. Everyone had heard the front door open and close. They turned their eyes toward the dining room door. In less than a minute, Eric and Josie were standing in the doorway.

Eric placed his arm possessively about Josie and drew her toward the group sitting and standing around the dining room table. "Ladies and gentlemen," he announced with undisguised love and pride in his voice, "let me introduce to you my lovely bride — Mrs. Eric Ford!"

Complete, shocked silence reigned a moment and then before anyone else could say anything, Joe strode forward. "I don't believe it!" he said belligerently. "Where could you get a marriage license at night?"

Eric didn't bat an eye, "There are ways to circumvent every obstacle if you are in love, my dear fellow," he said, and with a flourish he pulled a folded document from his coat pocket, spreading it out upon the table for all to see. It was indeed a marriage certificate which bore their names, announcing to the world that Josie and Eric were now husband and wife!

Clay grabbed Eric's hand in a solid grip, congratulating his friend. Linn threw her arms about a glowing Josie. Then Eric extended a hand to Joe and his tone was serious. "I hope we can be friends, Joe."

Joe was still scowling but he did shake hands briefly with Eric before he turned and sullenly left the room. Alfred was standing not far from Penny and suddenly his face lit up as he exclaimed to Penny, "That makes us almost kin!" Then he realized that everyone had heard him and he turned bright pink.

Mrs. Benholt had stood as if turned to stone during Eric's announcement and the congratulations. Linn saw that she was staring at Josie and Eric as if they were two

Martians who had dropped out of the heavens.

Suddenly Josie stepped away from Eric's side and kissed her mother lightly on the cheek with a soft, "I love you, Mom."

Mrs. Benholt was not a demonstrative woman and she seemed at a loss to know how to respond to her daughter's affectionate gesture. Then Eric moved to his wife's side and bent his tall frame, touching his lips to Mrs. Benholt's stern cheek. "It'll be nice to have a mother," Eric said earnestly. "Mine died when I was ten years old."

Linn was astounded to see tears gather in Mrs. Benholt's eyes before she turned and hurried away toward the kitchen. But at the door, Eric's mother-in-law abruptly turned around and said tartly to Josie, "Now you make that young man a good wife or you'll hear from me!" And she disappeared into her own domain.

"She likes you!" Josie said in delight to Eric.

"Of course! Old irresistible, that's me," grinned Eric. Turning to Clay he said, "Say, Boss, I could sure use a few days off for a honeymoon, if you could spare me." He grinned ruefully. "I'm afraid I've been a poor employee the past month, but I promise to reform from this day forth if I can have that week off."

Clay quickly agreed and Linn even volunteered to help at the office if her services were needed.

Josie hurried up the stairs to pack her suitcase.

Eric watched her go. "You know," he told Linn and Clay, "I tried hard to forget Josie, but the more I was in the company of that Sylvia person and a bunch of others like her, the clearer it became that Josie is a sweet, caring, genuine person, while the others are not worth a grain of sand.

"I'm deeply sorry for the way I treated Josie, but equally thankful for the time I spent with Sylvia. I needed her to compare a real person like Josie to. Josie is fine and honest and beautiful like a priceless gem. Beside her, Sylvia appears like glittering, cheap costume jewelry."

"Does Josie plan to go on to school and practice medicine?" Linn asked.

"Definitely!" Eric said. "We'll have to work out the details but I plan to finance the remainder of her schooling so she can devote her full time to study."

Eric drew a handsome salary as Clay's right-hand man and Linn knew he had invested his money wisely. Financing Josie's education should be no problem.

Before Clay left for the office, he sought out Alfred and told him he wanted to buy Alfred another ferret because he and Linn felt responsible for Baby's death, but Alfred told him no. "I'll be in college before too long," he said, "and I don't need a bunch of pets to dispose of. Mom doesn't care for pets, you know. But thanks awfully anyway!"

The next couple of days Linn went about her packing and sundry duties with a happy heart. Clay was setting things in order at the office and shortly after Eric and Josie returned, she and Clay would be heading for home. Grey Oaks! Now that the time was near, Linn could hardly wait to get there!

33

The day before they were to depart for home, Clay and Linn hosted an outdoor barbecue at Moonshell. All of the Benholts were invited, Stanley and Ellen Haskins, and Esteban Molinas and his wife, Alicia. And, of course, Josie and Eric, who had returned the night before.

Eric and Josie were so radiantly happy that even Joe began to lose some of his pessimism about their future together. He even admitted grudgingly to Clay that perhaps it might work out after all.

Mrs. Benholt had insisted on helping with the baking and her homemade yeast sweet rolls were a delectable accompaniment to the barbecued pork chops, baked yams, tiny pods of steamed okra, and a huge, garden fresh salad. Esteban had brought along a gigantic black diamond watermelon. The chilled slices of sweet, red melon were the perfect dessert to finish off the rich fare.

After the delicious meal they fell to discussing the hurricane and the smugglers.

"Well, at least you won't have to worry about Bonnie and Carlos any more," Eric said. "They're safely put away in prison."

"No, they aren't!"

All eyes turned in astonishment toward Esteban Molinas who had spoken the words.

Esteban lifted an expressive hand as if in apology. "I wish with all my heart that I could say Carlos was in prison!"

"So he got away scot free!" ejaculated Clay. "That sly fox!"

"You are right when you call him a fox," Esteban said. "Zorro means fox and that is what he is! But he came by it naturally; his father before him — Ricardo de la Zorro — was also a crafty old fox. Nothing could ever be proven, but the general consensus is that the fortune Ricardo amassed was from smuggling and other illegal activities."

His wife Alicia spoke up, "Both of Carlos's parents were from fine Mexican families. But old Senor de la Zorro was the black sheep of his family. Her family forbade her to marry him, but Carlota waited patiently for Ricardo to tire of the wild life he lived. Then she defied her family and married him when they were in their early thirties. Carlos is their only child and he has followed in the footsteps of his father, much to his mother's sorrow."

"What is his mother like?" Linn asked curiously.

"Carlota is still the fine woman — every inch a lady — that she was when she married Ricardo." Alicia sighed. "Loving Carlos's father seems to have been her only fault and she was loyal to him all their marriage until his death a year ago."

"How did Carlos manage to escape prison?" asked Eric.

"Money and influence, it seems," Esteban replied. "He produced witnesses that he — and Bonnie — had recovered those priceless artifacts from smugglers here in the States and were returning them to Mexico where they belonged."

"Unbelievable!" Linn said. "And they were caught with the goods!"

"Did you say Bonnie was also set free?" Clay asked. "We can't prove it, but that woman tried to murder my wife three times!"

"The witnesses exonerated them both," Esteban said sadly. "But at least I don't think you need to worry about their bothering you again. Carlos Rodriguez de la Zorro and Bonnie Leeds were married three days ago and apparently plan to live in Mexico at the grand and lavish Zorro plantation house, Guarida del Zorros — the Foxes' Lair, as the elder Senor Zorro whimsically named it. My brother came from Mexico last night and brought us the news."

"Bonnie and Carlos!" Eric said with a grin. "Two of a kind! I expect some fur will fly when the newness wears off that marriage!"

Suddenly Esteban stood to his feet. "Enough about those two foxes. I would like to talk about someone else." From his inside coat pocket he drew a pale green jewelry box. "I have here a little token for someone in this group who suffered a real loss a while back. Come here, Senorita Penny," he directed.

Penny got up slowly, her eyes wide with anticipation, and came to stand in front of Esteban.

Esteban's black eyes were twinkling as he opened the box and lifted a gold and jade necklace from its white velvet pillow.

Before he could unfasten the clasp to put it about her neck, Penny let out an ecstatic squeal, "My lizard necklace!" and began to jump up and down like a little girl instead of the thirteen-year-old she was trying hard to be.

"It's an iguana," Esteban corrected smilingly, "not a lizard. I'm sorry to say this isn't the same necklace as the one you lost. But I had a replica of it made by my brother who is a skilled Mayan craftsman and I doubt that anyone but an expert could tell the difference. He delivered it yesterday."

Penny stopped dancing up and down and lifted the small green iguana pendant, sighing blissfully. "It is so lovely." Then her face grew troubled as she looked up at Esteban. "But it must have cost lots and lots of money —"

"Chiquita mia, it did cost a good little amount, but what is money compared to the sparkle in those jade-green eyes of yours? Now, let's put it where it belongs, around that pretty little neck."

The remainder of the evening, if anyone felt any way but hilariously happy, he or she had only to glance at Penny's shining face to regain it.

Alfred looked somewhat crestfallen and told Penny woefully that he wished he could have been the one to restore the pendant to her. But she diplomatically responded that she would not have been given this one had it not been for the first one. Pacified, Alfred was content to bask in the reflected glory of Penny's gift.

Later that evening, after much congenial conversation and a songfest, Linn saw Eric and Josie slip away, hand-in-hand, to stroll on the gloriously beautiful, moonlit beach. Her heart felt full and joyous as she watched them go.

And, she observed the resentment and anger in Joe's eyes as he, too, watched Josie and Eric slip away. *Dear God,* she prayed silently, *help Joe to find you. You alone can fill the loneliness in his heart that the imagined loss of his twin sister has left.*

Linn turned toward her husband and Clay's hazel eyes met Linn's. He smiled. She felt his love reach out to her and enfold her in its embrace. Suddenly she wanted to be near him, feel the touch of his hand. She arose and crossed to his side and he moved over and drew her down beside him. All was well in her world and she was content.

Kissing Alice